"Come closer," he commanded.

The woman slowly, cautiously moved forward one step at a time. Her dark, tangled hair almost covered her face. When he could finally see her features, shocked amazement froze the words on his tongue. He could see the instant she recognized him, as well.

"Andronicus!"

Her voice came out in a breathless whisper that shivered through him. He'd thought he had gotten over his infatuation with this woman long ago, but his heart was telling him otherwise.

"Tapat! What… Why are you here?"

She glanced from him to the sword he still held tightly in his fist. He sheathed his sword, never taking his eyes off her familiar face.

She didn't trust him, not that he could blame her. He was a Roman, after all, and it was his people who now surrounded her city, embarking on a siege that would ultimately put an end to the world as she knew it.

His hands clenched and unclenched as he firmly held back the desire to yank her into his arms.

Books by Darlene Mindrup

Love Inspired Heartsong Presents

There's Always Tomorrow
Love's Pardon
Beloved Protector

DARLENE MINDRUP

is a full-time homemaker and homeschool teacher. Darlene lives in Arizona with her husband and two children. She believes romance is for everyone, not just the young and beautiful. She has a passion for historical research, which is obvious in her detailed historical novels about places time seems to have forgotten.

DARLENE MINDRUP

Beloved Protector

HEARTSONG
PRESENTS

Recycling programs for this product may not exist in your area.

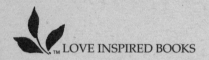 LOVE INSPIRED BOOKS

ISBN-13: 978-0-373-48704-2

BELOVED PROTECTOR

Copyright © 2014 by Darlene Mindrup

www.Harlequin.com

Printed in U.S.A.

The heavens declare the glory of God;
the skies proclaim the work of His hands.
—*Psalms* 19:1

To Allen, my beloved protector

Chapter 1

The Arabs called it *khamsin*. The Jews called it *sharav*. Andronicus didn't care what it was called; the effect was still the same. The fierce winds hit swiftly carrying a thick blanket of sand across Jerusalem and the surrounding vicinity. He pulled his cape around his face as the intense hot air blasted across his skin in rippling waves, threatening to peel the very skin from his flesh. Fortunately, he had made it as far as the caves in the mountains surrounding Jerusalem. Sliding his hands along the limestone walls, he eventually reached an opening and ducked inside.

He and his men had been on a scouting mission, searching out Jewish zealots and sicarii, when the storm had hit, separating him from the other members of his troop.

Sicarii were by far the most dangerous enemies he had encountered in his time here in Jerusalem. They were knife wielders who hid among the crowds and struck anyone they considered to be sympathetic to Rome. He had decided long ago that he was not going to be one of their victims and was ever vigilant. In this land, there were few who were not enemies of Rome.

After the violence of the tempest outside, the inside of the cave was eerily quiet except for the muted sound of the ongoing storm. As he continued deeper into the interior, he gave a sigh of relief at the cooler temperatures. Pulling off his helmet, he brushed the sand from the plume and tucked it under his arm. He glanced quickly around the dim interior and, seeing no imminent threat, began brushing the sand from his cape, his curling black hair and his clean-shaven face. Pulling his water flask from his belt, he swirled a mouthful of water to remove the grit clinging to his teeth and spat it on the ground.

As his eyes adjusted to the dimness, he took a more careful inspection of the interior of the cave, searching for possible hidden enemies, two legged or otherwise. The only light came from the opening behind him, leaving most of the cave in darkness and shadows. His soldier's instincts immediately went on alert, telling him that he was not alone; he could feel a presence just beyond his sight. The hair tingled on the back of his neck in warning. He placed the helmet back on his head, searching the small cave and noting two large boulders that could well hide a man. Every muscle in his body tensed in preparation for battle.

He slowly pulled his sword from its scabbard, metal scraping against metal in the silence.

"I know you're in here. Show yourself!" he commanded.

For the past several months, the besieged city of Jerusalem had shown its ability for terror. Even among the German barbarians he had never seen such viciousness. The zealots had wreaked havoc, especially against their own people inside the city. Rome had never fought an enemy so cruel, and Andronicus was in no mood for pity.

No movement or sound met his demand. Using the walls of the cave to protect his back, he advanced carefully toward the nearest boulder. With a quick thrust, he jabbed his sword behind the stone, the clang of the metal striking against the stone's surface and not a human body. Stirring from behind the other boulder warned him seconds before a figure darted toward the entrance.

Moving quickly, he slashed his sword across the entrance seconds before the figure reached it. With a yelp, the assailant skidded to a halt and, moving faster than Andronicus thought possible, scurried back into the shadows. He hadn't even had time to get a look at the person.

Adrenaline pumped through his body, setting it on fire with the rage of battle flowing in his veins.

"Come out now, or I will kill you like the coward you are." He spoke in Aramaic, his voice dangerously low, but surprisingly the figure answered him from the shadows in Greek.

"I am no coward. Please, I want only to leave."

The dulcet tones could only belong to a woman. Surprise rendered him temporarily speechless.

"Please," the woman pleaded, "I mean you no harm."

Andronicus hesitantly lowered his sword, something in the woman's voice cooling his blood to where he could think more clearly. For weeks, people from inside Jerusalem had been led by starvation to sneak outside the city to search for sustenance in the surrounding shrubbery. Usually they were caught, and Titus had crucified them on crosses close to the walls of Jerusalem—where those behind the walls could see them. Those who made it back inside the walls were killed by the zealots for anything they had managed to pilfer. But someone had obviously made it through the legions of troops and to this cave.

And something was oddly familiar about the woman's voice. His heart started thrumming in a way it hadn't for a very long time.

"Come closer," he commanded.

The woman slowly, cautiously moved forward. She was ragged and unkempt, her size giving the impression of a child rather than a woman. Her dark, tangled hair almost covered her face. When he could finally see her features, shocked amazement froze the words on his tongue. He could tell the instant she recognized him, too.

"Andronicus!"

Her voice came out in a breathless whisper that shivered through him like shards of ice and increased his heartbeat tenfold. He thought he had gotten over his infatuation with this woman long ago, but his heart was telling him otherwise.

"Tapat! What… Why are you here?"

He stared at her in utter amazement. He couldn't believe this was the same woman who had dressed in fine linen and moved with the grace of a gazelle. She looked more like something from the rat-infested sewers of Rome.

She glanced from him to the sword he still held tightly in his fist. Taken aback by her sudden appearance, he had completely forgotten that he was still brandishing the weapon. Recognizing her trepidation, he gave her a forced smile to reassure her while all kinds of questions swirled through his head, much like the swirling chaos outside. He sheathed his sword, never taking his eyes off her familiar face.

"I…I…"

Her answer was interrupted by a dry, hacking cough. Her tongue darted out to lick parched, chapped lips. His narrowed gaze focused on this telltale sign of dehydration.

He unhooked his water flask and handed it to her. With a grateful look, she quickly upended the goatskin and took a long draft, the water trickling down her throat. With a long sigh of relief, she handed it back to him with shaking hands. Instead of taking it, he asked, "How long have you been without water?"

She dropped her eyes to the ground. "Two days."

Andronicus's lips thinned with displeasure. "Two days! Have you been in this cave that long?"

A person could die of thirst in three days, two in this heat. He could tell she didn't want to answer. She didn't trust him, not that he could blame her. He was a Roman, after all, and it was his people who now surrounded her city, embarking on a siege that would ultimately put an end to the world as she knew it.

He glanced out the entrance and realized that the sandstorm was not going to abate anytime soon, a fateful intervention he was suddenly thankful for. It would be madness for either of them to try and leave. He looked back at Tapat, a million questions churning through his mind. His hands clenched and unclenched several times as he firmly held back the desire to yank her into his arms.

"It looks like we're going to be here awhile. Why don't we sit down and talk?"

The suggestion was met with a look of pure dread. What was it she was so afraid of? They had known each other for years, and although not really friends, surely she knew that he would never hurt her. She hesitated only a moment before nodding her head in acceptance and dropping to the ground at her feet. He could see the trembling of her hands where they clutched the skirt of her dirty and torn tunic.

Andronicus leaned against the boulder, his arms crossed over his chest, willing himself to remain calm.

She again tried to hand him the water flask she was gripping nervously, but he shook his head.

"Go ahead. Drink some more."

She did as he suggested, sighing with relief from a throat that had to surely be parched from the intense desert heat. He studied her bent head for several seconds. Her hair was dull and matted; he had never seen it thus. Each time he had seen her she had been well-groomed. He could still remember the scent of the rose water she used.

Now that they were together, his brain was too rattled to know how to proceed. It had always been so whenever he was in her proximity. To begin their conversation, he asked her the least innocuous thing he could think of to set her mind at ease.

"Have you heard from Anna lately?"

She jerked her head up, narrowing her eyes suspiciously. He sighed heavily. Obviously, the question was not as inoffensive as he had hoped.

"Tapat, I'm not seeking information about Christians. I'm asking only as a friend."

She relaxed slightly, but he could tell her guard was still firmly in place.

"I have not heard from Anna for some time. Have you?"

Anna had married his friend Lucius several years ago. Tapat had been a servant in the home of Lucius's mother, Leah. Andronicus's contact with Tapat had been minimal, but she had left a lasting impression. His friend Lucius had accused him of being in love with her. He didn't think it was that, but he had definitely been enamored of her. The erratic beat of his heart told him that it hadn't forgotten despite his not having seen her in years. Not since the night six years ago when she had saved his life.

The memories came flooding back. He had just returned to Jerusalem, having been sent back by Nero, who wanted him to use his spies to search out those who were fighting against Rome. He had promised Lucius and Anna that he would find Tapat and make certain that she was all right.

It had surprised him that Tapat hadn't gone with Lucius and Anna when they left for Rome, but Lucius had told him that she had responsibilities in Jerusalem. The look his friend had given him had warned him to ask nothing else. That, of course, had only piqued his interest further.

It had taken him some time to find her. She was living in a small house in the lower quarter of the city where many of the other Christians lived. His appearance at her door hadn't exactly been the wisest thing he had ever done, but he had been set on seeing her as soon as possible. It hadn't really occurred to him that his arrival would throw suspicion on Tapat in an already volatile city.

He never had found out what Tapat's responsibilities were, but then he hadn't exactly had time. Things in Jerusalem had become intense, especially after General Cestius Gallus had laid siege to Yodfat and then marched on Jerusalem. No one knew why the general had turned back, but it had increased tensions in the region. The whole area was one hotbed of hatred. And now Titus had moved his troops to surround the city and finish what Gallus had not.

Tapat had come to him one night at the Antonia Fortress shortly after his arrival. Her courage surprised him; he never imagined that she would even come near the place. He and his soldiers were supposed to go out the next day and Tapat warned him of an ambush.

He had been sent back to Rome shortly after that incident and had only returned now with General Titus. He hadn't seen her again, until today.

He looked at Tapat now sitting on the ground at his feet. Face tilted upward, her dark brown eyes were luminous from the reflected light entering the cave's entrance. She was a tiny little thing, standing only as tall as his heart. Her looks were so ordinary she would easily be overlooked in a crowd; some would call her plain, yet he had never failed to notice her. Whenever she was around, his eyes attached to her like the magnetic stones he had brought back from Germania.

"Andronicus?"

He snapped back to the present, one brow lifted in question.

"I asked if you had heard from Anna or Lucius."

He shook his head, not only to answer her question, but to clear it of the invading memories. "No. No, I have not. They left Rome when the persecution of Christians began."

Tapat's eyes darkened with anger. "I heard about the atrocities being perpetrated upon the Christians."

That would explain her reluctance to confide in him. He met her look squarely. "I helped them to leave."

He saw her shoulders relax. They studied each other for several seconds, each trying to think of something more to say. He had so many questions that he didn't know where to begin. Finally, Andronicus leaned forward, his eyes intent.

"Why did you disappear? I wanted to thank you for saving my life and the life of my men, but when I went back to your house, you were gone and you never returned. I know because I paid someone to watch for you."

Her eyes widened at this declaration. She stared into his eyes as though trying to see past them and into his mind. Whatever she was searching for eluded her. Sighing softly, she looked away. "I knew that they would come searching for me. The zealots have spies everywhere and they would have surely seen me at the Antonia."

"Where did you go?"

She looked up at him and smiled, though he could tell the smile was strained. "It's not important."

He wanted to argue with her, but one thing he knew about Tapat—she would tell him nothing that she didn't want to.

"Why are you still here in Jerusalem? I heard that the Christians had left some time ago. From what I gather, most of them have settled in Pella in the Decapolis region. Why did you not go with them?"

That look of panic was back in her eyes, making him go cold all over. What was she so afraid of? She couldn't possibly think that he would betray her. Or could she?

"I wasn't able to at the time," she told him reluctantly.

There it was again, that mystery that always seemed to surround her. Had other things not gotten in his way, he would have discovered her secret by now. Like a dog gnawing at a bone, he wouldn't give up until he finally knew what she had always kept hidden. He frowned, realizing just how ruthless that made him sound but, frankly, he didn't care.

"Why were you not able?"

She met his look of determination and, after several seconds, sighed in resignation.

Tapat stared at Andronicus and felt the reviving of those feelings she had thought long dispelled. She had been in love with him for years, this bold soldier of Rome. It did no good to berate herself. Her heart had never forgotten him, though his physical image had faded over the intervening years. Its intense throbbing reminded her of that now.

He was as handsome as ever, though his face bore the harsh lines of his profession. His dark hair and sun-bronzed skin were set apart by the glowing cinnamon color of his eyes. Those determined eyes were staring at her now, demanding an answer, and she knew the time had come.

"I couldn't leave my mother," she finally answered him.

His lips parted in surprise. "I thought your mother was dead. Isn't that why you were working as Leah's servant?"

She looked down, unable to meet his compelling stare. It was time to tell him the truth even though he would probably shun her as everyone else had.

And what did it matter anyway? Andronicus could never be anything to her. He was a soldier of Rome, an enemy of her people. More to the point, his life was one of heathen hedonism. If she had thoughts of anything between them, she had best forget them before she wound up with a broken heart.

"My mother was a leper in the Valley of Lepers several miles from here."

It had taken great courage to push the words past her lips, but the relief of it made her thankful that she had finally found the strength to admit it to him.

The silence that followed was profound. She chanced a peek at him and saw that his mind was trying to assimilate what she had just revealed to him. Instead of horror, she saw confusion.

"I don't understand. You were a slave when Leah bought you."

Her pulse was pounding in her ears. He wasn't looking at her with disgust but, rather, pity. She was thankful that he hadn't withdrawn from her after her revelation; still, she didn't want his pity.

"When the priests told my mother that she had leprosy, everyone we knew withdrew from us, even my father. He tried to take me with him, but I ran away and went back to my mother. He was too afraid to come after me. Without my father's support, we had no way to live, so I sold myself as a slave to a man in the city who hadn't heard of my mother's disease, and I used the money he paid me to secretly care for her."

He studied her thoughtfully. "Yet, you have no sign of the disease."

She shook her head, once again not meeting his eyes. "After I sold myself, my mother was so upset that she decided to live in the leper colony rather than be a burden on me or possibly infect me. It took me days to find her." Tears filled her voice. "As though she could ever be a burden," she added heatedly.

There was a long pause.

"You said she *was* a leper?" His soft voice held sympathy. "Did she die?"

Tapat's throat was choked with a grief that was still too

new. She nodded, fighting to suppress the tears that wanted to undo all the feelings she had firmly held in check.

"Two days ago," she choked out. Despite herself, a lone tear escaped and slid down her cheek.

At Andronicus's low growl, she looked up.

He reached down and pulled her into his arms, holding her head against his chest. The metal plates dug into her cheek, but she barely noticed.

"Go ahead and cry," he told her hoarsely.

She resisted but a moment and then surrendered to the grief she had been holding at bay for the past two days. Her eyes let forth an unceasing river of misery and pain, pain that had been with her ever since they had been banned from the Jewish community years ago. His other arm wrapped more tightly around her waist. It was as though he was trying to take the hurt from her and onto himself.

Eventually, there were no more tears left to fall. Grief spent, she hung limply in his arms. He continued to stroke her back in a way that brought comfort and security. It had been so long since she had had anyone to lean on, and it felt good to be able to relax and surrender to his care.

"What will you do now?" he asked softly.

"I don't know," she murmured. She would be content to stand thus the rest of her life. "There's nothing for me in Jerusalem now. I'll probably go to Pella."

She felt him tense. "Alone?"

She glanced up at him and blanched in surprise when she found his face so near. Realizing the precariousness of the situation, she pushed out of his arms to put some distance between them. His reluctance to let her go mirrored her own, but she had learned long ago that she could only depend on herself and Elohim.

She met his gaze with one of determination. "I *am* alone. I have been for years. I can take care of myself."

He lifted a brow dubiously. "Do you have food and money for this journey?"

"I have money," she answered. "I will go into Jerusalem and buy some food before setting out."

He shook his head. As he took her by the shoulders, she swallowed hard at his suddenly fierce expression.

"There is no food, Tapat. Titus has allowed people into Jerusalem, but he will allow no one out. If you go in, you will be killed. The zealots will think you a spy. Either that or you will starve to death like those people you see hanging on the crosses outside of the city walls. Many of them snuck out of the city, desperate for food, even to eat the grass growing around the city, and were caught."

She had been hearing stories of what was happening in and around Jerusalem, but living so close to the leper colony, they had been just that—stories. Dodging her way through the hordes of Roman soldiers between the Valley of Lepers and Jerusalem had made the stories all too real. She had had no idea of where she was going or what she would do when she got there, but she had to make it to this cave, where she had stored most of the gold Leah had given her. But gold would do her no good without food and water.

Releasing her, Andronicus brushed a hand back through his hair in agitation.

He turned back to her. "Don't go into Jerusalem. Stay here. I'll find a way to get some supplies to you."

Suddenly afraid for him, she placed a hand on his arm. "That's not necessary, Andronicus. I don't want to cause trouble for you."

He placed his hand over hers, squeezing gently. The heat from his calloused palm traveled up her arm and then slowly warmed her entire body. When their eyes met, something passed between them that left her too shaken to acknowledge.

"It's no trouble," he told her roughly. "Promise that you will wait here for me, even if it takes a day or two."

He took a small bundle from his belt and handed it to her along with his water flask.

"It's not much, but it will keep you from starving and thirsting."

She tried to hand it back to him. "What about you? The heat from the *sharav* can quickly kill a man without water."

He closed her hands around the containers and wrapped his own hands around them. "I am not far from my camp. I can get more. Take it, and promise me you will wait."

She nodded reluctantly. "Very well. I will wait."

She followed his look to the entrance of the cave and realized that the storm had abated without their notice. He released her hands and lifted a palm to cup her cheek. He stared hard into her eyes for several long seconds. When he spoke, his voice was husky.

"I'll come back soon. I promise."

With that, he picked up his cape from the floor of the cave where he had dropped it. Giving her one last look, he disappeared outside.

Chapter 2

Tapat watched from the entrance of the cave as Andronicus scrambled down the hillside, sucking in a breath when he nearly lost his footing. How many times had she watched those broad shoulders and that muscled physique and wished for something that could never be?

The man could have been a model for one of the many statues of Mars, the Roman god of war, which she had once seen in Caesarea. He stood head and shoulders above most of the men of her acquaintance, his powerful muscles attesting to the many years of service spent wielding the sword at his side.

He turned and glanced back at her, a black forelock falling from beneath his helmet, and even across the distance she could feel the magnetic pull of his cinnamon-colored eyes. He motioned with his head for her to go back inside. Nodding, she turned and retreated into the cool interior.

She went to the boulder she had been hiding behind and removed the sack of gold she had buried beneath it. Her former mistress had given her this gold before she left for Rome, and although she had made use of it to care for her mother and the others in the Valley of Lepers, she still had much of it left.

She opened the bag and pulled out a smaller bag containing a dried flower that was beginning to crumble from its rough handling over the past few days. She gently stroked a finger over the dried blossom, remembering when Andronicus had given it to her. He often came to the villa to see Lucius, and that day he had startled her in the peristyle.

"Hello, Tapat."

Tapat had whirled at the voice, one hand going to her chest as she sucked in a sharp breath.

"Andronicus! You frightened ten years from my life."

How could a man as large as he move with such stealthy grace? The thudding of her heart had changed tempo when he came closer. He had grinned.

"I suspect it wasn't my fault. You seemed to be a million miles away."

That was certainly true, though she would never have shared with him why it was so.

"Are you looking for Tribune Lucius? I think he is in the bibliotheca."

Andronicus then glanced toward the library but turned back to her. He'd moved closer and she'd taken a hasty step in retreat, almost tumbling into the garden's fountain. If not for his quick reflexes, she would have made a complete fool of herself.

He didn't immediately release her, and the warmth of his touch had tingled through her and brought swift color to her face. Her eyes had widened in fear, not of him but of her reaction to him. Seeing her look of distress, he'd released her.

"Th…thank you."

"My pleasure." The timbre of his voice had given a

meaning to the words that was hard to miss, even for someone as naive as she.

He then took a hibiscus blossom from the bush next to the fountain and placed it behind her ear, allowing his hand to slide down and cup her cheek.

What would have happened next, she would never know. Self-preservation had made her pull away even though she longed to stay. She had fled from the garden as though the hounds of Hades were after her.

Tapat sighed and came back to the present. So many things had happened to her in the past two days that her mind was still trying to make sense of the confusion. She didn't even know where to begin. She had prayed to the Lord for protection and deliverance, and He had sent her Andronicus. How ironic.

When the zealots overthrew the Roman soldiers at the Antonia Fortress in Jerusalem a few years ago and then took over the city, she had managed to escape through one of the myriad tunnels that wended their way under the city.

She had needed to be near her mother, and nothing was going to stand in her way. Not the zealots. Not even the whole Roman army.

Jesus had given His disciples a warning of events to come and when the signs began to be fulfilled, everyone had left the city. Everyone, that is, except her. She couldn't leave her mother no matter how dangerous it might be to stay.

Even from this hill one could see the many crosses standing before the city of Jerusalem, reminding her of what Andronicus had just told her. Her people were literally being starved to death. As they escaped the city, Roman justice was swift and sure. Tapat knew without a doubt that it was only by her Lord's protection that she had made it to the safety of this cave, and that safety was tenuous. She ached from the pain and loss that those crosses represented.

She settled herself on the cold ground and opened the bag of supplies Andronicus had given her. Roman soldiers carried enough supplies on them to last for three days, but what she found in the bag would last *her* much longer. Even after two days she still had very little appetite, her grief being still too new. But she couldn't allow her body to weaken if she hoped to make the long trek to Pella.

Taking a handful of corn, she munched on the kernels as she tried to decide what to do next. She had promised Andronicus that she would remain here, but what if something happened to him? How would she even know? She couldn't stay here indefinitely; someone was sure to find her.

A lizard ran across the floor and up the far wall of the cave. Tapat smiled.

"There you are. Where did you disappear to?"

The small reptile had kept her company for the past couple of days. She had seen no sign of him all day and wondered if something had happened to it. Despite the fact that reptiles were considered unclean animals, the little creature had made her feel just a little less lonely. It cocked its head slightly, keeping a wary eye on her.

"Don't worry. I'm not going to hurt you."

She began a rambling conversation that included everything from the treachery of the zealots to her mother's death, winding up with that astonishing moment when she had come face-to-face with the only man she had ever loved.

Were anyone to hear her, they would surely think her a lunatic, especially conversing with a lizard. She smiled wryly to herself. Loneliness could make a person do some strange things.

She felt the loneliness more keenly now, knowing that her mother was no longer there to care for. She had no one now. Her father had died several years ago of fever. Strange that her mother had outlived the man who had been responsible for shunning them from the Jewish community. When Tapat learned of his death, she had felt nothing but pity.

A noise outside the cave alerted her that someone or something was coming. Surely Andronicus couldn't have made it to his camp and back in such a short time. She quickly rose, intent on seeking refuge behind the boulder, when a form blocked the light from the cave entrance.

Andronicus had scrambled down the hillside, his thoughts in chaos. How was he to make good on his promise and get Tapat to safety? Roman troops surrounded the countryside for miles around, and if that weren't bad enough, beyond them were the mercenaries, paid killers, situated to effectively block the exit of anyone who managed to slip past the Roman forces.

His mind tried and rejected several ideas.

Why, oh why, hadn't Tapat left the vicinity with the other Christians? Surely her mother would have understood. But then, no one he knew was as fiercely loyal as Tapat. She would gladly die for someone she loved.

That thought brought him up short. Could that have been why she forewarned him of the ambush awaiting him and his men? She cared for him enough to ignore decorum and seek him out where she had no business being seen. He didn't even want to think what she must have been doing to be privy to the information she had brought him.

He made it back to camp and immediately searched out the men who had gone with him on his scouting expedition. They had become separated in the storm, and he wanted to make certain that they had returned safely before he made preparations to return to Tapat.

One of his centurions was awaiting him at the entrance to his tent, his relief evident when he saw Andronicus.

"Tribune! We were about to send out a search party."

The centurion followed Andronicus into his tent. Andronicus dropped his helmet, sword and gladius on the mat he used for his bed. He reached for the pitcher of water sitting on the table by his bed and poured some over his head, relieved by the cool moisture. Taking a cup, he splashed water into it and thirstily drank it down.

"Have Arius and the others returned yet?"

"Some have returned. A few are still missing."

Andronicus jerked around. Although he felt concern for his men, he was more concerned with their discovering Tapat. "How many?"

"Five. Arius is one of them."

Andronicus felt a sinking sensation in his midsection. Arius was more than one of his soldiers; they had been friends for years.

"Thank you, Nonius. I will see to gathering some men to search."

"General Titus wished to see you as soon as you returned."

Antonius nodded. After Nonius left his tent he blew out a breath. Now what? More than likely Titus had some job for him to do that, knowing the general, was going to take more time than he had originally anticipated.

Tapat, please have patience and don't try to leave.

After washing the sand from his body, he picked up his helmet, sword and gladius and made his way to Titus's tent. He found the young general surrounded by his other tribunes. They turned at his appearance.

"Andronicus." The general gave a brief jerk of the head in acknowledgment, his searching eyes going slowly over Andronicus. "We were beginning to worry."

Although younger than Andronicus by six years, Titus was a formidable presence at the age of thirty-one. Many a man had made the mistake of underestimating the general's youth. He had proved himself campaign after campaign as more than a boy. He was a fierce, intelligent and deadly opponent. There wasn't a man here who wouldn't willingly follow him into battle.

"The storm, my lord," Andronicus answered. "It hit without notice."

Titus grunted. "This lousy heathen countryside. Give me the green fields of Rome any day."

There were several murmurs of agreement.

"Now," Titus declared, turning back to the map spread out on the table. "Let us get down to business." He glanced up at Andronicus. "You missed all of the action."

"Sir?"

"While you were gone, those infernal Jews figured out a way to destroy our siege engines and then had the audacity to attack our camp."

Andronicus wasn't surprised. These zealots were either very foolish or very determined. They had no compunction about killing even their own people if it suited their purposes. From those Jews they had captured outside the city, they had learned of horrible atrocities being perpetrated upon Jews in the city, who had done nothing to warrant such attacks. The brutality of the Jewish leader, John, was beyond anything Andronicus had ever faced.

"We should bring the full force of our army against them," Tribune Sestus growled. "If we had done so in the beginning, this war would be over by now. We have the men, so why not use them?"

"They have the advantage of the high walls. Many of our men would die needlessly," Tribune Marcus rebutted. "Let us build the siege engines again. It will take time, yes, but it will also save lives."

Titus glanced at him. "And where would we get the supplies to build them? We have already stripped every tree around here for miles."

"Perhaps," Andronicus suggested, "if we tighten security around the city walls…"

"We already tried that," Sestus argued, "and they still manage to sneak through."

Titus turned to Andronicus, his dark eyes glinting. "You had an excellent idea, Andronicus, about keeping the men occupied. If we are going to prolong this siege, then to make it work, we need to fortify our defenses."

That was the very reason Andronicus and his men were out scouting the hillsides. Laying siege to a city was a tedious, time-consuming business and when men had too much time on their hands, problems from boredom usually arose. He tried to keep his men busy to avoid any such possibility.

"Since so many people are still leaving the city to scrounge for food in the area outside the city, and since we know that supplies are being smuggled into the city somehow, we are going to build an earthen siege wall around the entire city."

Andronicus knew exactly what *we* meant.

"How soon do you want us to begin?" one tribune asked.

The general stood and glanced at each one of his soldiers. "Right now, Quintas. Give the order to your centurions."

Slamming their fists against their chest in salute, they quickly exited the general's tent.

Andronicus found one of his centurions and gave the order. He knew the men were bound to grumble, but they would still respond with deadly enthusiasm. Anything to limit this siege and allow them to return to their homes.

The men set to with a will. At the rate they were going, it was going to take less time than Andronicus had originally anticipated but still longer than the time limit he had given Tapat. He could only pray that she would do nothing foolish, like try to set out for Pella on her own. She was bound to be spotted if the *sharav* heat didn't kill her first.

He needed to find a way to get her some supplies and get her out of here, and he needed to do it now.

He backtracked his way to Titus's tent, intent on somehow finding a way to be relieved of duty for a short period. No matter what he could think of to say, it was still going to seem suspicious, his wanting to leave now. Still, it was going to take some time to build the siege wall and still longer to wait out the city's starvation.

He heard a commotion outside the general's tent. Andronicus had to forge his way through a barricade of packed soldier bodies to make it to the entrance. He could hear Titus's raised voice speaking to someone inside, and he didn't envy the person who had incurred his wrath.

When he ducked inside, he found out what all the tumult was about. Arius was standing at Titus's side and Tapat was kneeling before Titus's feet, eyes focused on the rug she was kneeling upon. Andronicus felt his heart cease momentarily then drum at the speed of a racing chariot. His eyes sought the general's face, and his breathing almost stopped at the intense look of rage there.

"I will not repeat myself again, woman. Answer me!"

It took great courage for Tapat to lift her face and, with great deliberation, shake her head at the general's command.

"I have told you the truth. I am no spy."

When Titus lifted his hand to strike her, Andronicus, knowing the power behind that arm, was released from the shocked stupor Tapat's sudden appearance had generated. He quickly stepped forward and stayed the general's hand by gripping his wrist. Surprised, Titus glared at Andronicus.

"My lord, I know this woman."

Although the anger never left Titus's face, he relaxed somewhat at Andronicus's statement. But the eyes that met his held a warning, and the pointed look he gave Andronicus's hand gripping his brought his instant release.

"She was found hiding in a cave near here," Titus growled. "What do you know of this?"

"He knows nothing," Tapat interjected quickly.

"Silence, woman," Titus bellowed. He turned back to Andronicus, his look one of suspicion. It was not surprising that he would be doubtful knowing that there were spies among them, and Titus was not known for showing mercy to spies.

"This woman saved my life and the life of my men. I owe her." He met the general's look head-on without flinching. He was a soldier of Rome, but he would not back down on this issue regardless of the threatening looks thrown his way.

Titus glared at him for several long seconds before he motioned around the tent.

"Leave us."

Surprised at the command but conditioned to obey, the others left quickly. Only Titus, Andronicus and Tapat, still kneeling at the general's feet, remained.

Titus leaned against the table displaying the map of Jerusalem. He folded his muscled arms across his broad chest and glared at his tribune and then his captive.

"Explain."

The very softness of the command warned of feelings held tightly in check.

Andronicus did so in as few words as possible. When he had finished, Titus gave him a peculiar look.

"I see. And what exactly would you have me do with her?"

Andronicus took a deep breath before meeting the general's eyes. "I would like to see that she gets safely to Pella, just north of here."

Titus glanced from Tapat to Andronicus. "Perhaps…if she is willing to give us some helpful information."

Tapat looked up at him, the fear in her eyes evident, yet her voice was firm when she answered him. "I have already told you. I know nothing."

Andronicus willed himself to appear unconcerned. "My lord, she is after all but a woman."

He ignored the flash of anger that darkened Tapat's eyes, his lips twitching as he hid a grin. If not for Titus's presence, he had no doubt that she would let him know in no uncertain terms what she thought of such a statement.

Titus stared at Tapat for a long moment, his expression unreadable. "Don't forget, Andronicus, that Rome was built on the backs of treacherous women."

Although that was indeed true, Andronicus thought it wise to remain silent. He wasn't certain what Titus saw when searching Tapat's features so diligently, but the air suddenly left him in a rush.

The general looked at Andronicus, but he couldn't begin to interpret what he saw on his commander's face. "A soldier always honors a debt," he agreed.

Andronicus didn't even realize that he had been silently petitioning Tapat's God for His intervention until he fervently thanked Him in his mind.

"As soon as the siege walls are finished, you may take a few men and escort the lady to Pella," Titus told him. "I don't expect the siege to last long, and I will need you here when we begin our assault of the city."

Titus's narrowed eyes settled on Tapat once again, but he spoke to Andronicus.

"Have one of your men take the woman to your tent and see that she stays there. I would have a word with you."

Andronicus slammed his fist against his chest in salute, glancing briefly at Tapat. He went to the tent opening and called Arius inside.

"Take the woman to my tent and see that she remains." He cast his friend a speaking glance.

Andronicus's eyes connected with Tapat's as she passed him. *Trust me,* he told her silently. She warily eyed the general before giving a quick nod to let him know she understood.

He watched her walk away, hoping that he could live up to that trust.

Chapter 3

Andronicus faced his superior, fairly certain what was on Titus's mind. The inside of the tent was lit only by the burning braziers and what little light penetrated from the opening. The planes and shadows on the man's face masked his youth, making it look as fierce as when he marched into battle.

Titus glanced at Andronicus, one eyebrow lifted. "You are one of my finest soldiers, Andronicus. Are you certain you understand where your priorities lie?"

Deciding that the best defense was a quick and effective offense, he told Titus, "I will not deny that I have feelings for the woman, my liege, but they do not surpass my love of Rome."

He wasn't exactly certain that what he had just said was true. Rome was slowly killing itself with its depredations and its constant thirst for more power. Andronicus had become increasingly weary of the incessant battles to procure more land for an empire that was having a progressively hard time holding on to the lands it had already conquered.

Titus went to a table in the corner and lifted a small bag. Coming back to stand before Andronicus, he opened the bag and allowed several gold coins to fall into his cupped palm.

"And how do you explain these? Arius confiscated them from the woman. People in the city are starving and money is scarce. How came she by such a fortune if not for information she has been giving the enemy?"

Andronicus knew about the money that Leah had given Tapat, but he hadn't realized that it was a small fortune. At least he could clear up *that* misconception. He explained about the bequest Leah had given to Tapat and her reasons for doing so.

He didn't miss Titus's skeptical look. Frankly, he couldn't blame the general. This whole situation was enough to twist a person's mind. Titus studied him from under lowered brows.

"I heard that Tindarium had married a Jewess. But as for you, Tribune, there is a reason that legionnaires are forbidden to marry. Rome will not tolerate divided loyalties."

"I understand, sir, but my honor will not allow me to neglect so great a debt as what I owe this woman. And not only me—several of my soldiers are indebted to her, as well. *Dictum meum pactum.*" It was the truth. His word was his bond and he would never go back on it.

Titus stared at him for several long seconds and Andronicus willed himself to remain still under that stern scrutiny. If Titus doubted Tapat's innocence in the least, her life wouldn't be worth a mina. Seemingly satisfied, Titus relaxed.

"As I told you already, the men will be building a siege wall around the city. I foresee it taking several weeks. Once that is completed, you may repay your debt. In the meantime, the woman is your responsibility."

Andronicus didn't miss the implied threat and, once again, slammed his chest in salute. He then hastened from the tent before the young officer could change his mind.

Tapat paced the small confines of Andronicus's tent. What was she to do now? Andronicus's look implored her to trust him, and she did, but the same couldn't be said of his general.

When brought to Titus's tent, she was amazed that he was so young, but one look at his face told her he was no callow youth. Young in age he might be, but his features told a different tale of a seasoned warrior. If all of Rome's army was like him, Jerusalem didn't stand a chance.

She worried her bottom lip with her teeth. The soldiers who found her in the cave had confiscated her gold. Without that gold, she wasn't certain how she would survive. But right now, that was the least of her worries.

Oh, she knew the Christians in Pella would see that she wanted for nothing, but she hated the thought of being beholden to anyone. Besides, the weekly collection was for those who were destitute or unable to work. She didn't consider herself to be either, but that was something she would work out when she got to Pella. *If* she got to Pella.

She glanced around the inside of the tent, noting that Andronicus was as meticulously clean with his quarters as he was with his person. She had always admired that about him.

As evening was falling outside, the illumination from the braziers lessened. She huddled closer to the one that lit the area surrounding the sleeping mat, instinctively feeling the need to be closer to the waning light.

The tent was bigger than many that surrounded it but not nearly as large as the general's. Titus's tent was grander than most of the homes her people lived in. No expense had been spared for Emperor Vespasian's son. Her mouth had watered at the selection of food sitting on a table in the general's quarters, and she realized that for the first time in days, she was hungry.

Tapat picked up the pitcher of water on the table and poured herself a cup. After quenching her thirst, she sat down on the bedroll, pulling the pillow up and hugging it to her chest in an unconscious need for security. Andronicus's scent lingered on the pillow, the mixture of man and sandalwood pleasant and, somehow, calming.

The only other items in the tent were a large chest sitting against the far wall, a small table at the bedside and the braziers set systematically around to provide light where it was most needed. The Spartan quarters fit his personality.

Her curiosity aroused by the chest, she was tempted to go and open it when Andronicus entered the tent.

She quickly pushed the pillow aside, embarrassed to have been caught cuddling it, and got to her feet.

"You are to remain here until the siege wall is built," he said, glancing sideways at her.

Did he mean here in this tent? Her eyes widened in apprehension and she swallowed hard. Seeing her concern, he came close and took her by the shoulders. She had to look a long way up to read what was in those deep brown eyes.

"I will stay with Arius in his tent," he told her reassuringly, and the dread she had been feeling lessened. This was Andronicus; he would never hurt her. Would he? But what did she really know about him? Only that he was a very integral part of Rome.

She was startled at the fierce look that unexpectedly filled his face, especially in lieu of her earlier thoughts.

"I know it will be hard for you. This is not what I had planned."

"It's what Elohim has willed," she told him softly, knowing with complete trust that it was the truth.

He stared at her for a long moment before heaving a

deep sigh and releasing her. He turned away and went to the chest against the wall. "Your God is a confusing god," he told her, a decided edge to his voice.

Tapat thrilled to the fact that he was at least acknowledging Elohim. She had been praying for this soldier of Rome for a very long time. If only he would come to know her lord as his friend Lucius had. She had rejoiced for Anna when she'd received word of Lucius's conversion to the Way.

"Our scriptures tell us to trust in the Lord with all our heart and lean not on our own understanding. If we knew all the reasons for everything that happens in this life, we would be God."

"I suppose that is true," he acknowledged reluctantly. He glanced at her and his eyes held a question. "So your God has willed that you be here with me?"

Tapat's heart responded to the throatiness of his voice and drummed an ever-increasing beat. "So it would seem."

The look he gave her made her want to run from the tent, but that would be like jumping from the pot into the fire. What was he thinking that darkened his eyes to obsidian? She shivered in an unconscious response.

He gave a soft snort, opened the lid to his trunk, reached inside and pulled out a small leather sack. He brought it over and handed it to her.

"It's not as much as what Leah gave you, but it should help you to get settled."

She opened the sack and found it full of silver coins. She looked up at him in surprise.

"I cannot accept this!"

He frowned in annoyance. "Why not? You accepted more than that from Leah."

How was she to explain the difference to him without being offensive?

"Leah's was a gift." *Of love,* she told him, but only in her thoughts.

Casting her look to the ground so that he couldn't read what was in her mind, she tried to return the sack, but he pushed it back at her.

"As is this," he told her. The look on his face was meant to quell any desire to argue, and it took more strength than she realized she possessed not to capitulate.

"Leah's was a gift of love for the years of service I gave her." She pushed the bag into his hands again.

"And this is a gift to repay that which Rome has stolen from you," he rebutted, trying to give it back.

Tapat placed her hands behind her back. "It is not your debt to pay."

Various expressions chased across his face. He cupped her cheek with his palm, rubbing his thumb across her lips, and all desire to argue fled.

"Do not forget the debt I owe you. Surely you would agree that my life is worth more than these few coins."

She could not argue differently, for no amount of money would make up for his life.

"Do not fight me on this, Tapat," he told her huskily. "You will not win."

The words of Solomon came suddenly to her mind. *A gift opens the way for the giver.* She had given Andronicus the gift of her protection and he was returning the favor. It would be churlish to refuse, yet her pride was her worst enemy. But then, how could she ever repay her debt to Christ for all He'd done for her? A gift given in love should be accepted in the same way, even if that love was what the Greeks called *phileo,* a brotherly love, whereas hers had been more what they called *eros,* a woman's love for a man. She reached out and took the bag, her eyes meeting his.

"Thank you, Andronicus."

A look of relief crossed his face and he dropped his hand to his side. They continued to stare at one another until a rap on the tent brought their attention to the man standing at the entrance.

He glanced from one to the other, a smile twitching at his lips. "It's time, Tribune. Titus has gathered the troops."

"I'll be with you momentarily."

Andronicus turned back to Tapat. "Stay in this tent. No matter what, do not go outside. Understand?"

She nodded, swallowing down panic at the thought of him leaving.

"I will return as soon as I am able to take you somewhere where you can take care of nature's call, and then we will sit down and have a meal together."

She nodded again, surprised at his insight, and then he quickly disappeared outside.

Tapat took the bag he had given her and slowly crossed to the trunk. She clutched the bag with both hands, holding it against her chest as she tried to get up enough courage to open the trunk and return the coins to their proper location.

Before she had been piqued by curiosity to peer into the trunk, but she now realized that that would be an invasion of his privacy.

She gently laid the bag on the top of the trunk and returned to the sleeping mat, relieved, as she was once again surrounded by the circle of the brazier's light.

It bothered her to sit so idle. Before, she had always had something to do to occupy her thoughts. Now, they threatened to burst forth from the confines of her mind that had always firmly held them in check. She did the only thing that she knew to do, the only thing that always seemed to help calm her mind: she prayed.

Andronicus gave his orders to his centurions, who then passed them on to his troops. He looked around him at the looming walls of Jerusalem and realized what a daunting task this was going to be. Building siege walls was always a tedious and time-consuming business, but what it took in time, it saved in countless lives.

Titus was right about one thing, though: it would certainly keep the men from becoming bored with waiting out the holed-up zealots. They were fighting men and not used to being idle. When not in battle, they were either training or carousing. Sitting still was something they thoroughly detested.

The men set to with a will that surprised Andronicus. They were not particularly enamored of the more mundane physical tasks they were often asked to perform. Still, the sooner the project was completed, the sooner the city would become weakened. And the sooner the city became weakened, the sooner they would be able to scale the walls with less resistance. And then the battle would truly begin.

He wasn't certain if it was the desire for battle that spurred the men on, or the knowledge that the sooner this city fell, the sooner they would return home.

But to what? A brief respite before they were sent out to battle more enemies? The life expectancy of a soldier of Rome was very short. It was one of the reasons that soldiers couldn't be taller than a certain height. It saved in the cost of uniforms to be able to pass them along once a soldier died. The thought made Andronicus suddenly ill. He looked around at the faces of his men and wondered how many of them would never make it home. For that matter, would he?

This thought brought Tapat vividly to his mind. He had to get her someplace safe before the fighting began. If he didn't survive…

He pushed the rest of the thought away. It didn't bear thinking about. He surprised his men by grabbing a charred timber from the burnt siege engines and helped to lift it onto the growing wall of debris.

Sweat poured from their faces in the hot summer heat, yet each man worked industriously without complaint. The walls that Titus had originally thought would take weeks would be finished far sooner.

Andronicus decided that he was not needed here any longer and so removed himself to his tent. His heartbeat accelerated with each step that brought him closer to his destination. He paused outside, taking a deep breath to calm his nerves before entering. The thought of the coming invasion didn't stir his nervous tension as much as the woman who awaited him inside.

He found her curled up on his sleeping mat. Her even breathing told him that she was sound asleep.

Stepping quietly, he made his way to her side and knelt next to her. He reached out a hand to touch her but stayed the impulse, not wanting to awaken her. It was much easier to study her with her guard down.

One small, calloused hand was curled under her cheek, the other clutching his pillow against her chest. The innocent picture she made caused such a surge of protective instinct he could barely breathe.

Although he had always seen her as a rather plain little thing, her face in repose had a peace that transcended the mere physical. Perhaps that was what had always drawn him to her. He hungered for such peace himself but, as a soldier of Rome, that was something he had never been able to find. He knew that it had something to do with the religion she embraced. He had seen that same peace time and time again, even with people facing roaring lions. Even his friend Lucius demonstrated that same kind of peace after embracing this Christian religion.

Her dark hair was matted after having not seen a comb in days, its dullness, he felt sure, due to a lack of sustenance. Before her hair had hung long and glistening down her back and he had often had to stifle the urge to touch it. Even with it lank and tangled, he found himself still stifling that same urge.

He wondered, not for the first time, what she would look like in a colored toga, her hair intertwined with ropes of pearls. Realizing that his breathing was becoming constricted, he shook off such fantasies and touched her gently on the shoulder.

She awoke with a start, clutching the pillow more tightly to her chest. As awareness dawned, wariness crept into her eyes once again. She slowly sat up, rubbing the sleep from her eyes.

"Are you hungry?"

Her wide, blinking brown eyes reminded him of the roe deer that roamed the region.

"I am, a little."

His lips twitched. That had to be the greatest understatement of all time. After several days without food, she had to be more than a little hungry. Her body was thin to the point of emaciation.

He continued to study her until he saw the color blooming in her cheeks at his close scrutiny. He got swiftly to his feet and held out his hand.

"Come with me. I know of a small wadi where you can wash up if you wish. There's not much water in it now, but there should be enough, and it's somewhat private."

She gave him a look of relief and placed her hand in his. He pulled her to her feet, not releasing her immediately. They stood holding hands, each searching the other's eyes for something neither was fully aware of.

His own growling stomach reminded him that it had been some time since he had eaten, as well. He smiled wryly.

"We had best hurry. Daylight is fading fast."

As they navigated the circuitous route of the camp, soldiers stopped what they were doing to stare. It was not uncommon for women to follow the soldiers, but they were prostitutes looking for easy money. Even in the outermost reaches of the empire, the emperor always managed to pay his troops. Wise, since that was what the security of Rome depended upon.

Whenever a man studied Tapat too long, Andronicus gave him a glare that soon sent his look elsewhere. He knew that the men must be thinking that Tapat was his personal concubine, but it was better that than that they try to approach Tapat whenever he wasn't around.

He bit back a smile at their obvious surprise. He was known for choosing his women from those who were of the highest caliber of cleanliness. They must surely think he was desperate, but he could stand the slight to his reputation as long as it protected Tapat.

He led them onto a path that took them away from the nearest campfires. When they reached the edge of the wadi, Andronicus stopped Tapat with a hand on her arm.

"Wait here until I clear a path."

He moved forward with caution, using his spear to stir the brush around the flowing water in case a snake or some other miscreant might be lingering in the vicinity. When he was satisfied, he motioned Tapat forward. He met her look, his eyes holding a warning.

"Be careful. I will be farther back to give you some privacy, but I will be close enough. Call if you need me."

Nodding, she moved past him and knelt by the water. He watched her a moment and then moved away.

Chapter 4

Tapat knelt at the edge of the wadi and plunged her hands into the cool, running water. Crickets sang their cadences around her, mingled with the faint voices of the soldiers coming from the camp in the distance.

Because of the intense heat of the *sharav,* few wadis still had running water. She wondered how this one had been spared. Thanking Elohim for this extra blessing, she began rubbing the water over her arms and face.

Oh, how she longed for the warm baths of her former mistress's villa. That time seemed so long ago now that it was more like a dream than a reality. If not for the gold that had been given to her and had helped to pave an easier path, she might have thought she had dreamed that former life.

The water wasn't plentiful enough to fully bathe, but she relished the feeling of the cool night air touching her exposed wet skin. If only she had a way to wash her tunic. She felt so dirty, especially beside Andronicus. How did the man remain so clean amid all this dirt?

And her hair. How long had it been since it had seen a good washing? Leaning farther out into the water, she was able to duck her hair below the surface enough to get it thoroughly wet. She scrubbed at her scalp, doing the best she could with nothing to clean it with. Beggars couldn't be choosers and this would just have to do.

Andronicus's voice came to her from the darkness.

"We need to go back now, Tapat."

She wrung the water from her hair. It might not be completely clean, but it felt much better.

"Coming."

She finished her ablutions and hurriedly made her way back to Andronicus's side. His glance passed quickly over her, and his lips tugged up into a smile.

"Feel better?"

She returned his smile. "Much."

He lightly gripped her arm and headed them back to the camp. She tried hard not to notice the looks of the men as they passed through the camp, but she couldn't help but register their astonished expressions. She sighed inwardly. She could hardly blame them. She must look like something that a dog had dragged through the streets.

When they reached Andronicus's tent she was surprised to find that a meal was waiting. A thick rug had been laid on the floor with food set out on plates in its center. She hesitated, glancing quickly at Andronicus. He motioned to the rug.

"Have a seat."

She seated herself cross-legged on the rug and Andronicus took his place across from her. She studied the food and then gave Andronicus a speaking look that he obviously read very well.

"No, soldiers do not always eat this well. The extra rations are because of Titus, the emperor's son."

Whatever the reason, the food made her mouth water.

Bowing her head, she gave thanks to Elohim for the bounty and for His care. When she opened her eyes, Andronicus was watching her.

"Tell me about this God you serve," he demanded softly. He handed her a platter, allowing her to choose her own food.

She began filling her plate, trying to decide the best way to begin. How did one describe the Creator of the universe in just a few sentences?

"What exactly do you want to know?"

Andronicus filled his own plate and shrugged. "I don't know. What makes you so certain that your God is the only god there is? For that matter, what makes you believe there even *is* a God?"

Tapat frowned, thinking carefully before reaching for the subject he would most likely respect.

"Your gods, and those of other heathen nations, cause chaos among themselves and the people who serve them. This is not the world we live in." She hesitated, but he nodded for her to go on.

"Our world is a world of order. Everything Elohim created is for a purpose, and it fulfills that purpose efficiently. Only mankind disrupts that order. When we follow His commands for our life, we find the peace that brings order."

Andronicus had stopped eating and stared at her with narrowed eyes. "And how is all of this part of that order?"

He motioned around him and she realized that he was talking about the war on Jerusalem.

"God sent His Son to bring peace to the world, but the Jews have rejected Him."

His brown eyes sparked with an inner anger that she didn't understand.

"And those who didn't reject Him, what of them? Where was your God of peace when they were in a Roman arena being torn apart by lions?"

She shivered at his graphic description. Sighing, she was fairly certain she would never be able to explain such a thing to his satisfaction. Greater Christians than she had tried...and failed. It was something that was understood by the heart; another thing he would probably never understand.

"He was there," she told him adamantly. "The kind of peace I speak of is not the same as what you are envisioning. I do not mean a world without war or hardship, but a people united with Elohim. The word we Jews use for *peace* means a repair of something that was torn apart. It means that the relationship that mankind once had with Elohim has been put back together by Christ's blood."

He sat back, his food forgotten.

"So, you're speaking of a peace that comes from within."

She nodded her head. "Yes. The Messiah Himself told a story of two men who built their houses, one on sand, another on rock. Neither one was free from storms, but the one on rock stood firm. He has not promised us a life without problems, only that He will stand by us when those problems come."

Andronicus once again concentrated on his food. "That makes sense," he agreed. "How exactly did this relationship with your God get torn apart?"

She began at the beginning and, as briefly as possible, explained Elohim's plan of salvation from the Garden of Eden to Christ's death on the cross. As always, there was a catch in her throat when she tried to explain the crucifixion, tears hovering just near the surface.

"And the Jews in Jerusalem don't believe this?"

She shook her head sadly. "No. Those who accepted the Messiah fled when the signs our Lord warned about began coming to fruition."

"To Pella," he stated.

She hesitated. It had only been a few years since Nero

had waged war on Christians, trying to eradicate those he considered a threat to Roman tolerance. If Andronicus knew of the whereabouts of the Christians, were they then in danger with Rome?

He read her thoughts. "I am no danger to you, Tapat, nor to your fellow believers," he told her quietly.

"And Rome?"

He shook his head, resuming his eating. "Rome has more problems than it can deal with right now. Your fellow believers are safe for the time being."

That, at least, was good to know.

They finished their meal in silence. Tapat took the goblet of wine he handed her and stared into its ruby-colored depths. She was not used to the rich, fruity drink. She was much more accustomed to the *posca,* the watered-down wine of the poor. One more thing to show just how far different she and Andronicus were.

"What are you thinking about so hard?"

She jerked her head upward at the softly spoken question but decided to be honest. "I was thinking about how different we are."

He frowned. "Not so different," he disagreed. "Other than the fact that I am a man and you are..." His voice became husky as he studied her once again. "You are definitely a woman."

Tapat went cold all over at his look and then her cheeks heated with color. She turned her attention back to her plate to break the connection with those arresting cinnamon-colored eyes.

Andronicus recognized her trepidation. In truth, she had a good reason to be afraid. The longer he was in her presence, the harder he had to fight with his baser instincts. Another thing the Roman army had done for him. It was hard to maintain any semblance of humanity when touched by so much depravity day after day.

He got to his feet and went to his trunk. Opening it, he rummaged around inside until he found what he was looking for.

Coming back to Tapat, he dropped a comb into her lap. She jerked back, glancing up at him in surprise.

"I thought you might like to have that," he told her. He then placed a blue tunic made of soft linen next to her. "And that."

She stared at him in amazement, and no little amount of disappointment, and it didn't take much deliberation to realize that she was thinking he had acquired them for a mistress.

"I purchased them in Caesarea for my sister," he told her. "I can get her others and I think perhaps you need them more."

At her belligerent look, he shook his head, his own face setting with grim resolve. "Don't argue."

Their silent battle of wills lasted several moments before Tapat finally dropped her gaze and picked up the soft garment. She glided her hand across the surface before glancing at him again.

"It would be nice to be clean," she capitulated reluctantly, and he allowed himself to relax.

A servant came to remove the leftover food and the blanket. Tapat got to her feet, clutching the garment to her chest. She finally met his look with one of appreciation.

"Thank you."

He nodded. "I will have some water brought to you so that you can fully cleanse yourself. I know there wasn't much you could do at the wadi. I just thought it might be nice for you to be free from camp for a few moments."

He took the cruse of olive oil that had accompanied

their meal from the departing servant and handed it back to Tapat. She slowly reached out and took it.

Picking up his cape from where he had laid it, he fixed her with a look meant to relieve her of some of her anxiety. "I will be close by."

It took every ounce of strength he possessed to leave that tent with her sitting there looking so lost and afraid.

He made arrangements for the water to be taken to her and then made his way to Arius's tent. The other man was already reclining on his own bed. He motioned to the mat that had been prepared across from him.

"Come in and join me, my friend."

Andronicus ducked inside, shaking his head at the disorder. His friend was not as fastidious in his cleanliness as he. Andronicus supposed, as his leader, he could always order him to clean the place up, but because Andronicus was invading the other man's privacy, that would hardly be appropriate.

He placed his helmet and gear neatly on a table sitting nearby. "I appreciate your sharing your quarters."

Arius shrugged. "I do not mind." He studied Andronicus for several seconds. "Why don't you just sleep with the woman? It's obvious that you want to, and it's equally obvious that she is in love with you."

Andronicus jerked around, his anger quickly surfacing. He had already put that particular thought to rest; he didn't need it resurrected. Tapat was incredibly innocent and it would be so easy to seduce her, but if he ever did, he knew without doubt that he would lose all respect for himself.

"Watch it, Arius. We are old friends, but you are treading into an area that doesn't concern you."

The surprise on Arius's face quickly cooled Andronicus's anger, which was more at himself than the other man. It wasn't like him to be so defensive. He pulled off his chest piece and carefully laid it aside. The piece was special to him, having been a gift from Lucius. He glanced at Arius, stifling the swirling emotions causing him such chaos. "I apologize."

Arius smiled wryly. "Not necessary. I didn't mean to pry."

"I know. That's why I apologized."

Arius sat up, wrapping his arms loosely around his bent knees. He studied Andronicus curiously. "At the risk of being flayed alive, can I ask you something?"

Andronicus felt himself tense. "If you must."

His friend was not deterred by the less-than-friendly glare Andronicus threw his way.

"What exactly do you see in this woman? I have watched you turn away some of the most beautiful women in the empire, yet this one brings out something in you I have never seen before."

They had been friends too long for Andronicus to be offended. He had wondered the same thing often enough himself.

"I don't know. Lucius and I discussed it often."

"Tribune Tindarium?"

Andronicus nodded, and Arius again relaxed back against the cushions.

"That's another one I have often wondered about. When I first saw his wife I thought her rather homely, but then, after they married, it was almost as though a veil was removed from my eyes. She is actually rather striking."

Andronicus had thought much the same thing. He grinned. "His wife told me that it's Lucius's love for her that makes her different." He finished removing his gear, sat down on his sleeping mat and unwound the leather leggings of his sandals.

Arius's look was skeptical. "I have never seen love do such a thing."

Shrugging, Andronicus told him, "Perhaps your idea of

love and hers are two different things." He lay down, rejecting the covers in the stifling heat.

"If you say so," Arius returned, getting up and snuffing out the braziers one at a time until the tent was in darkness.

After settling himself into his bed, Andronicus lay with one arm behind his head and stared through the open doorway into the night. Several feet away lay the woman they had just been discussing. The last thing Andronicus remembered before sleep claimed him was the thought of those incredible dark eyes.

Tapat made use of the water Andronicus had provided. She had snuffed out all but one brazier before stripping the soiled clothes from her body and washing with the supplies that accompanied the water.

The scent of the sandalwood soap reminded her of Andronicus. Although she had loved him for a very long time, she had always been afraid of him, as well. The conflicting thoughts and feelings had made her cautious of the man.

Now she was even more leery. She recognized that predatory look in his eyes. She had seen it often in men, their eyes following women on the street. It amazed her that Andronicus's look had been centered on her. How was this even possible? Had he been so long without a woman that any woman would do?

She had heard stories of Romans and their debauchery but never the details. She had never been taught the ways of men, and this left her somewhat vulnerable, but she had seen enough in her life to know that she needed to move with caution.

Plunging the soap into the basin of water, she tried to focus her thoughts on more practical things, like what she was going to do when she got to Pella. She had no doubt that she would get there because Andronicus had given his word and she had never known him to fail.

After cleaning herself thoroughly, she felt refreshed for the first time in days. The last time she had washed was three days ago, just before her mother died. The reminder brought back the stinging pain of her loss.

She slid into the soft tunic Andronicus had provided for her. It glided over her body like silk.

She crossed over to where Andronicus had left his shield lying against the trunk. Turning it around, she studied her distorted image in its polished surface. At least she looked less like a beggar from the streets of Jerusalem.

Sitting down on the sleeping mat, she tucked her legs under her and began using the olive oil and the comb Andronicus had given her to work the tangles from her matted hair. How had he known that she needed the oil for just such a purpose? As handsome as he was, his knowledge of women must be extensive. The thought, coming just after the reminder of her loss, left her depressed. It would be better for her to remember that her purpose in life was not tied up with this admittedly intriguing soldier of Rome.

When she had combed her hair to her satisfaction, she used the towel to wipe the extra oil from her hair. It left it soft and shiny, once again giving her a feeling of satisfaction, which then caused her to chide herself at her preoccupation with her less-than-flattering looks.

She was reminded of the Apostle Paul's warning to women about being so focused on their looks that they forgot that their beauty was to come from inside in the form of a godly heart.

"Forgive me, Lord," she whispered.

She took the basin of water, intent on emptying it outside. When she pushed back the flap of the tent, she almost dropped it. A soldier stood guard outside the doorway. He came to instant attention, his eyes widening in surprise at her changed appearance.

He glanced at the basin in her hands, then back at her.

He shifted his spear to his other hand and, reaching out, took the water from her. "Just leave it. I will see that it is taken care of."

Tapat swallowed hard, releasing the basin to him. Was she then a prisoner, or was the guard for her protection?

"Thank you," she told him and scurried back inside.

When she lay down for the night, her swirling chaotic thoughts caused a tear to trickle from her eye only to be followed by a sudden deluge. She couldn't get her mind to focus long enough on one idea to know just what to pray. In the end, she merely sighed three words. "Help me, Lord."

Chapter 5

The sun was just beginning to rise over the Kidron Valley when Andronicus tapped on the entrance to the tent to let Tapat know that he was about to enter.

He found her sitting cross-legged in the middle of the sleeping mat, her changed appearance making him pause midstride.

The servant entering behind him almost collided with him and struggled to balance the food in his arms. Andronicus stepped out of his way quickly, his eyes never leaving Tapat as she gracefully rose to her feet.

She no longer looked like a ragged street urchin but more like the nubile young woman he remembered. So concerned had he been for her safety, he hadn't really paid attention to the scent of her unwashed body. Now the fragrance of sandalwood assailed his senses and his nose flared in appreciation.

"I thought we could share the morning meal," he told her, trying to steady the beat of his thrumming heart.

She merely nodded and he was aware that something had altered in her since the last time they were together, though he couldn't put a name to it. She again seemed leery of him, so he tried to put her at ease.

"I brought bread and fruit, which will be left for you so that you can have something the rest of the day. I will not be back before the evening."

The servant once again laid the blanket in the middle of the floor and placed the food on it. He glanced briefly at Tapat, then quickly left. She watched him exit the tent and turned burning eyes to Andronicus.

"Is he a slave?"

Andronicus shook his head, moving to the blanket and seating himself. "No. He is a personal servant who goes with me on my deployments."

She joined him on the blanket, handed him a platter and gave him a questioning look.

"His name is Nasab. I saved him from the Germans and now he feels he owes his life to me no matter how many times I tell him otherwise. It's a belief of his people."

He began to load food onto his plate as he studied her curiously. Her fiery look told him that she did not approve of slavery. He was intrigued.

"You do not approve of slavery, and yet your own people owned slaves and you sold yourself as a slave."

She glanced at him in surprise. "The difference is that one was of a willing nature."

"Are all Jewish slaves of a willing nature, then?"

He didn't know why he was goading her, but it irked him that she had such a low opinion of him.

She frowned. "No, but if slavery is done in accordance with the laws Elohim gave Moses, it lasts but a short time and is only supposed to be in desperate situations. God's law allows freedom after seven years."

His look was skeptical. "And of course your people follow these laws in detail."

She had the grace to blush. "No, they rarely do," she admitted. "Just like most of Elohim's laws, the people have forgotten. They choose to ignore His word and then they have to pay the penalty."

"It's the same with every civilization," he told her. "My people are no different."

They retreated into silence as they consumed the morning meal to break their fast. The sound of the camp waking and stirring about outside penetrated into the lasting quiet. The prolonged silence was making Andronicus uneasy.

He continued to study Tapat but surreptitiously so that he wouldn't make her uncomfortable again. Her hair now hung in a glistening, silky black stream down her back and, although she was still much too thin, the light blue tunic was becoming against her dark skin.

She glanced up at him, a seeming veil over her eyes that no matter how hard he tried, he could not penetrate.

"I am not used to being idle," she told him. "Is there nothing that I can do while we wait to leave for Pella?"

He chose some grapes from the fruit bowl, adding them to his plate. If it was hard for his troops to sit idle during a siege, how much more so for a woman used to being of service? Still, he could think of nothing that would relieve her tedium.

"I'm sorry. I know how monotonous the waiting can be, but there is nothing that you can do here that wouldn't involve your leaving this tent, and that is forbidden."

She nodded, dropping her eyes once more. The silence continued between them unabated until Andronicus finished his meal and had no more reason to stay. He got to his feet, putting on his helmet and sword that he had laid aside earlier.

He reached down and tilted Tapat's chin until he could

see her face. He studied her features, trying to find some semblance of the woman who had come to him that night years ago fearing for his life.

"Have patience," he remonstrated softly.

She smiled faintly. "That is not one of my virtues."

He returned her smile, releasing her. "Nor mine.

Andronicus stopped at the tent entrance and turned back to her. He opened his mouth to say something but then could think of nothing that would be of benefit. Her very silence forbade any further delving on his part.

Ducking outside, he made his way to where the troops were already beginning the work of increasing the siege wall.

Dozens of faces stared at them from the outer wall of Jerusalem, some full of hate, others full of fear. Periodically, arrows rained down upon them, sending the soldiers running for cover, but the accuracy of their shots was minimal because of the distance from the city.

The zealots tried to jeer the Romans into an angry attack, but the soldiers were too well trained for such a ruse. They ignored the jibes and steadily worked at increasing the siege wall, knowing that it was only a matter of time before they would be able to seek vengeance.

Andronicus stared in amazement at the amount of work that had already been accomplished on the raising of the wall, marveling at his men's initiative. Nothing motivated troops more than sheer boredom and a desire for revenge.

Already the wall was several feet high. What Titus had thought would take weeks to accomplish looked, at this rate, as if it would be finished in days. Perhaps he would be able to get Tapat out of here in a much shorter time than he had originally anticipated. He glanced at the blue sky above him and wondered if such timing had anything to do with her God.

Already the sun was a burning disc in the bright morning sky. The sweltering heat of the day was going to make the work of lifting and placing stones that much more grueling, especially when the men had to do so in full battle gear.

After seeing the men well started on their labors, Andronicus then retrieved his horse and, joining the other tribunes, made an inspection of the entire wall rising around Jerusalem. Soon, the people of Jerusalem would be cut off from any escape route and thus would begin the real siege of the city, a siege meant to starve the people into submission. Many in the city had desired to give in to the Romans and were killed by the Jewish zealots, who were determined to fight to the end.

Thus began the pattern of his life for the next few days. During the daylight hours he oversaw the building of the wall, in the evening he spent time with Tapat, and when the hour grew late he made his way to Arius's tent to spend time staring into the darkness and thinking about the woman so close yet so distant.

The highlight of his day was when he would share a meal with Tapat during the evening hours. They began to relax in each other's company and started sharing bits of their lives with each other, but he could tell that she was holding back from him.

He was beginning to understand the woman a little better. After all she had been through, he marveled that she had remained so unscathed by all the evil that had touched her. It astounded him that she could still believe in this God of hers, yet she clung to Him with a fierceness that defied explanation.

She stood in the opening of the tent now, staring up at the stars in the night sky. The warm evening breeze ruffled the edges of her tunic and lifted the dark curtain of her hair. He could see her standing there, yet she seemed to be somewhere far away.

He couldn't even begin to guess what she might be thinking. Although she had relaxed around him to a small extent, she was still keeping most of her thoughts and feelings well hidden. He had tried to feel her out on certain subjects and she had closed up like the stopper on an amphorae.

He went to her, cupping her shoulders with his hands and noting with pleasure that she was finally putting on some weight. He felt her tense but refused to release her. In truth, he looked for any reason just to touch her or to be near her.

"The soothsayers say that our destinies are tied up in those little specks of light," he said to make conversation, following her look to the star-studded night sky.

She glanced over her shoulder, and the look in her eyes gave him pause.

"Is that what you believe?" she asked. Something in her voice told him that this was no idle question.

He stared into those lustrous brown eyes and wanted the moment to go on forever. He was here with her now; the evening was peaceful and he felt as though the outside world had disappeared entirely. He almost felt content.

"I believe we make our own destinies," he corrected.

"So you are your own god, then?"

He was having a hard time focusing on what she was saying when those lips were so near his own. He had to clear his throat before he could answer her.

"I would not claim so much power."

She turned back to again stare at the millions of twinkling lights. "Then who created all of this?"

He hesitated, knowing that this was not the moment to make some idle comment. This was obviously important to her.

He searched the glowing orbs in the sky and felt something move within him. Part of him wanted to accept that there was a god, any god, who actually cared about the lives of the people. But he had been to too many places and seen too many things to believe this was so. Before he could answer, she spoke again.

"The heavens declare the glory of God; the skies proclaim the work of His hands. Day after day they pour forth speech; night after night they display knowledge. There is no speech or language where their voice is not heard."

He shivered at the eerie cadence of her voice. She spoke almost as an oracle. He turned her around, his narrow-eyed look searching her face.

"Where did you hear this?"

She smiled. "It is in our scriptures. A psalm of our King David."

She pushed out of his hold and returned to the rug to finish her meal. He gave one last look to the stars and then followed her.

"I told you that we were different," she said. He had the feeling that although she was looking directly at him, she wasn't really seeing him. Just as in the doorway, she seemed distant.

He pushed his dark hair from his eyes and sighed heavily. Whenever they were together, he had to choose his words with care in order not to offend her in some way, yet whatever he said still seemed to be wrong. He got the distinct impression she was trying to put up walls between them that would be harder to scale than the siege walls that had today, finally, been completed around Jerusalem. Instead of months, it had taken four short days.

In the same amount of time, Tapat had had time to build her own walls.

He glared at her, wanting to tear away that shell of protection she had formed to hide her feelings. He was tempted to break that shell with a subtle seduction, to force her to admit her feelings, but he knew, as he had admitted to himself before, that that would accomplish nothing except his own downfall.

He knew without conceit that she was attracted to him, but she was fighting it with every ounce of her being, and, instinctively, he knew that it centered on her faith in her God. Her attempt to put barriers between them was playing havoc with his ability to think clearly.

He groaned inwardly. It was foolish to be having romantic thoughts anyway when in a short time he would be going into battle with the very real likelihood that he would be killed. If anyone should be putting up walls, it was him.

His anger evaporated as quickly as it had come.

"You're probably right. We are different," he acquiesced quietly and she jerked her head up in surprise. For just a second her guard was down enough for him to realize the pain he had just caused her. But her mask of indifference slipped quickly back into place.

He got to his feet and retrieved his gear. There were times when he just wanted to shake the woman.

"Titus has given us permission to leave tomorrow. It will be several weeks before our troops will be able to begin their assault, so I must return by then."

He could see the fear in her eyes. Fear for him or for her people?

"We will leave early, so get some sleep."

He waited for her to say something, but she merely nodded her head. Was she, like him, wondering just what their future would entail? Perhaps that was what had brought about his comment regarding the stars. It was a simple comment, yet it only succeeded in driving deeper the wedge between them.

"Good night."

He made his way to Arius's tent, stopping just outside and glancing once more at the starry night sky. What had she said? Something about the stars speaking of her God?

"If You're up there," he ground out, "remember that she loves You. Keep us safe on our journey."

The blazing star that shot across the darkness he took as a good omen.

Chapter 6

Tapat rolled up the blue tunic and placed it in the bag Andronicus had provided. She had washed her old tunic and changed into it in preparation for the trip to Pella. The journey would take them through many miles of desert before they reached the plains of Jordan, and she didn't want the tunic Andronicus had given her to be dirty and tattered when they arrived.

She added the comb and smiled wryly. Everything she owned in the world was in this little bag.

With great trepidation she had overcome her reserve and dared to open Andronicus's trunk and replace the silver coins he had insisted that she have—she refused to be so indebted to the man. Her upbringing forbade it.

A stirring outside her tent let her know that Andronicus was about to arrive. Every nerve in her body jumped to screaming life whenever he was near. It frustrated her no end that the man affected her so. Her life had been much simpler before he had come into it.

He tapped on the tent before coming inside. He noted the change of clothing with a lifted brow but said nothing.

Nasab followed Andronicus inside with the morning meal. He gave Tapat a brief smile before arranging the food on the rug. He and Tapat had become friends of a sort over the past few days. It was Nasab who had brought her food to eat and water for bathing.

Something about the man had reached out to Tapat and encouraged her, once she found out that he spoke Greek, to strike up a conversation. He had readily responded, which spoke of the man's loneliness. She wondered if Andronicus even realized that his servant was longing for home but was determined to do what he considered his duty by staying.

Nasab left and then returned carrying a garment over his arm. He handed it to Andronicus, who in turn handed it to Tapat.

"A shawl. I know how Jewish women feel about being seen without a head covering."

She wanted to object, but he was right. It would be unseemly to travel in the company of men and not be more modestly dressed. Because he hadn't retrieved it from the trunk, she wondered how he had come by it, but she didn't dare ask. She was learning that some things were better left unsaid and some gifts better taken without comment.

He then went to the trunk and removed the sack of coins Tapat had replaced earlier. He walked over to the bag that contained her tunic, opened it and dropped the coins inside. The look he gave her dared her to argue.

"Did you think I wouldn't notice?"

Her face warmed with embarrassment. "You have given me too much already."

"I thought we had settled that argument once and for all," he said.

Tapat took a slice of goat cheese and glanced at his set

face. She shrugged, knowing that he wouldn't give in. "It appears that we have."

She knew she sounded ungracious but she couldn't help it. She frowned at his grin. He knew he had won this particular battle, and that irritated her more than the fact that she had been caught.

He seated himself opposite her once again and began choosing food from that provided. She knew that once they left this camp and struck out into the surrounding countryside, the fare would become much simpler.

She longed to be free from this camp and all that it represented, and she certainly didn't want to be here when the true battle began, but, at the same time, she was reluctant to see the end of the trip they were about to embark on because it would mean she would no longer be able to see Andronicus.

The thought that he might be killed tore at her heart. But even if he did survive the battle, he would leave her in Pella and she would never see him again. Their worlds were too far apart. She knew this to be true, yet she couldn't stop loving him any more than she could stop breathing.

She had prayed to Elohim to remove that love from her heart, but He had steadfastly remained silent. It was a thorn she would just have to live with.

"How long will it take us to reach Pella?" she asked.

He dipped the last bite of his bread into the bowl of olive oil. "I'm not certain. Usually it would take us four days moving at a good clip. However, having to travel slower along the way will significantly impede our progress. Probably a week at least."

She knew without being told that she was the reason for the more leisurely pace. She didn't know whether to be thankful for the consideration or not.

Andronicus gave her a long look. "What will you do when you get to Pella? Where will you live?"

Tapat dusted bread crumbs from her lap. "I have friends there. They will help me find a place to live."

His only answer was a slight grunt. He was studying her again in that unnerving way. She cleared her throat nervously and began collecting the empty plates and stacking them for removal. "Will Nasab be going with us?"

He shook his head. "Not this time. I have duties for him here."

Nasab entered the tent to remove the empty plates and gave Andronicus an affronted look, assuring Tapat that the decision was not his idea. She would miss the old man. She gave him an understanding smile.

"May Elohim be with you, Nasab. I hope we will meet again someday."

The old man's eyes shimmered with tears. "And I you."

Andronicus glanced from one to the other, a frown drawing his brows together, and began to gather his gear; Tapat hastened to do the same.

A jingling of harness from just outside alerted them that the other soldiers accompanying them had arrived and were ready to leave.

Andronicus held the tent flap for her to pass through. She stopped abruptly, her eyes widening in alarm at the huge beast that was standing before her. She had to look a long way up to see the men mounted on their steeds.

She stared appalled at Andronicus, who was waiting patiently by one of the horses. He motioned for her to come forward so that he could help her to mount. She took a hasty step in retreat, shaking her head vehemently.

"I have never ridden a horse before. I have never even been on a donkey!"

His lips twitched. "All you have to do is sit on it. I will do the leading."

She swallowed hard. The horse was a magnificent animal, the color of the desert sand. But as impressive as the beast was, there was no way she was going to ride it.

Andronicus must have recognized the stubborn set of her chin because he walked over and in one swift movement lifted her into the saddle. She grabbed for the horse's mane, clinging like a leech. She couldn't decide if she was more angry or more frightened, but she didn't have time to do anything about either when the horse shifted beneath her, forcing her to cling tighter to his mane.

She glared at Andronicus's back as he turned away. The snickering of the other soldiers brought hot color to her cheeks and closed her mouth on the blistering words she was tempted to speak. She settled her shawl over her head and ignored them all.

Andronicus looked around at the other men who would be traveling with them. He could practically feel Tapat's eyes burning a hole into his back. "Are we ready?"

Arius slapped a fist against his chest. "Ready, Tribune."

Five men were not a lot to rely on if trouble did occur, but he would wager his months' worth of salt that these five he had chosen could outfight twice as many, if not three times as many, assailants.

His friend Arius was the only man who had ever bested him in practice combat. Germanic blood ran through his veins, and he stood taller than any man in his cohort, the bulging of his muscles speaking of his many hours of training. If any trouble arose, he wanted Arius there to guard his back so that he could focus on Tapat's safety.

The other four men were also some of his best. He had had his doubts about Crassus when he had first joined his command, but the young man had proved himself worthy over time.

Celsus, Salvius and Didius, despite being battle hardened, were prone to pranks often. Even now they were making sport among themselves, but one look from him and they settled into silence.

Nasab glared sulkily from the doorway of the tent. Andronicus would miss the old man, but he would only slow them down. It had taken a great deal of persuasion on his part to get Nasab to agree to stay behind. Although Nasab was a servant, he had become more like a friend. Andronicus saluted him with a finger to the forehead as they passed. "I will see you when I return."

The sun was just rising in the eastern sky when the group picked its way carefully through the many soldiers littered about the hillsides surrounding Jerusalem. More than fifty thousand men, along with horses, tents and equipment, darkened the hills and valleys.

The soldiers watched them pass by with only mild interest. When they had traveled for several miles, the crowd of campsites began to thin.

They ambled along at a leisurely pace until they were well outside the perimeter of Roman troops. Beyond lay the camps of the mercenaries, thousands of men who would kill their own mothers for money. Andronicus gave them a wide berth.

He glanced back to check on Tapat, riding just behind him. She met his look with one of pure venom. He bit back a smile knowing it would only infuriate her further.

Still, she was doing well for her first time on a horse. He hoped that as she adjusted, he would be able to pick up the pace. It didn't surprise him that with her natural grace, she had instinctively adjusted to the gait of the steed.

He turned back to keep watch on the terrain around them. Nothing moved except for several kites flying high in the sky. The birds were a sign that something was dead not far away. He moved farther out so that they would not be on an intercept course.

Whichever way he turned, his inspection was met by

a sandy, rocky terrain almost devoid of life. Dried foliage dotted the rolling hillsides, while other plants struggled to survive the scorching summer heat.

Celsus began to sing a song. His baritone voice was not unpleasant, though the words were hardly meant for a lady's company.

Andronicus turned and gave him a speaking look that dropped him into silence. Celsus glanced at Tapat in embarrassed understanding and then chose another song. It was still as bawdy, but because he was singing in Latin, Andronicus doubted that Tapat could understand the words. Celsus's intent, no doubt.

Andronicus still didn't appreciate the noise, as any brigands in the area would undoubtedly be drawn by the sound. Before he could remonstrate with the man, Arius turned on him.

"Quiet! Do you want every crazed zealot in the area to know where we are?"

Celsus glanced around hurriedly, a sheepish look covering his face. "Pardon, Centurion. I wasn't thinking."

Arius glared back at him. "Indeed. Remember that it will not only be your life if we are attacked."

A thoroughly rebuked Celsus retreated into silence, his attention now focused fully on the job at hand. Satisfied, Andronicus returned to studying the area. He wondered for the hundredth time how the people could be so devoted to this desolate land. As for himself, he longed for the green hills of Rome.

He glanced back at Tapat and thought that she had fallen asleep until he noticed the movement of her lips. She was praying to her unseen God. He glanced around nervously, almost expecting to see Him appear, but they traveled on in undisturbed silence.

The sun was beginning to descend when they reached the outskirts of a seemingly abandoned village. Such was the sight all over the countryside. With the coming of the Romans, villagers had fled their homes and headed for the seeming sanctuary of Jerusalem. Andronicus wondered just how many of these homes would never see their owners again.

If the place were truly abandoned, it would be the perfect spot to stay the night. The men dismounted, and he stayed with Tapat while they searched through the area for hidden enemies. When they were satisfied that the village was deserted, they nodded at Andronicus. Everyone except Arius had returned without incident. Andronicus began to relax.

He climbed from his mount and went to help Tapat from hers. She stared down at him tiredly, no longer full of the fight he had come to expect from her. She placed her hands on his shoulders, and he helped her to the ground.

She would have collapsed to the sand if his hands had not been spanning her tiny waist. He winced in commiseration.

"Your legs aren't used to riding and certainly not for such a long time." He tucked a strand of hair behind her ear, content to hold her for as long as necessary. "Are you all right?"

She nodded, pushing out of his arms. "I am well. Why have we stopped?"

He frowned at her rejection of his touch. "It would be better for us to stay here than out in the open."

They glanced around at what had once been a thriving little village. Not even so much as a chicken gave any sign of life.

"Tribune," Arius called from the far end of the village. The anxiety in his voice brought four swords swiftly sliding from their scabbards. Andronicus drew his own, pushing Tapat behind him.

The centurion made his way quickly to their side.

"We have a problem," he told Andronicus, and something in his voice alerted Andronicus that it was a problem that didn't require swords. He sheathed his and the others followed suit.

"Is the village not abandoned?" Andronicus asked.

Arius glanced briefly at Tapat. "Not exactly."

"What does that mean?" Andronicus asked him impatiently. He was tired and in no mood to play games.

"If you will follow me."

Arius started to lead the way and the others followed. Arius stopped, glancing once again at Tapat. "Perhaps it would be best if the others remain here."

Andronicus noted that warning tone again. He nodded at the others. "Watch over the woman. I'll return shortly."

He followed Arius until he stopped at a hut almost at the end of the village. A slight cough from inside warned Andronicus that the house was occupied. He glanced at Arius.

Arius pushed open the door to the hut and ducked inside. Andronicus followed, his gut telling him that he wasn't going to like what he found.

The first thing that hit him was the stench. He involuntarily gagged, stepping back to catch his breath. It reminded him of the dungeons below the arena.

The fading daylight coming in from the open doorway barely dented the darkness in the house. As his eyes adjusted, Andronicus could see Arius standing by a bedside and looking down. He was holding his cape across his nose to block the smell.

In the bed lay a woman and child. The woman was so emaciated, she looked like a skeleton with a thin layer of skin. He shuddered at the sight. Tapat hadn't looked much better when he had first found her.

Dull, glazed eyes stared up at them uncomprehendingly.

Andronicus pushed Arius aside and went down on one knee, struggling to overcome the stench.

He felt the woman's forehead and found her burning with fever. She was conscious, but barely.

The child lying beside her was a mere infant, still in swaddling cloths, which were soiled and reeking. The infant obviously hadn't been changed in days. It lethargically suckled at its mother's breast, so close to death that it could merely whimper in distress.

"What are we to do?"

Andronicus hesitated. They couldn't just leave them here to slowly starve, but he also didn't think they would survive for very long. He could understand why Arius hadn't wanted Tapat to see this sight.

"Tribune? The humane thing would be to put them out of their misery."

Before Andronicus could answer him, they were startled by a scream from the doorway.

"No!"

Chapter 7

Tapat had watched Andronicus walk away and had almost called him back. She, too, hadn't missed the inflection in Arius's voice warning of something that he wouldn't say outright. Why had the man looked at her like that?

The eeriness of the deserted village made her edgy. She could tell the soldiers felt the same. Their uneasy glances continually swept around the village and beyond. They kept their hands resting on their swords.

How sad that many of these homes would never see their occupants again. Would this little village cease to exist, along with so many others? Thousands of Jews had died already, and when the attack on Jerusalem commenced, many more would also. It saddened her to think that their rejection of the Savior had cost them eternity with Elohim. If it saddened her, how much more so Him who loved them so much He was willing to sacrifice His only Son?

Curious about the people who had lived here, she crossed to the house closest to her and, feeling like an intruder, eased open its door and peered inside. It was a typical Jewish home with clay walls and a dirt floor. Dust motes caused by the air from the opened door danced in the fading sunbeams coming from the room's lone window aperture. Whoever had once lived here had left in a hurry. Items were scattered about haphazardly, plates left on the table.

A rat scurried across, knocking over a lamp, and she jumped back in alarm. She quickly backed out and closed the door.

The house next to it was completely opposite. The owner of this house had set his house in order before leaving. Except for the dust covering every surface, the place was neat and tidy. Very little furniture and few home goods had been left behind, suggesting that they probably had someone with whom to stay in Jerusalem, or else they had moved farther east where Rome's presence had little been felt.

Tapat's vivid imagination could picture the chaos that erupted when news of the Roman invasion reached here: people running about, children crying, animals squawking as they were being caged for travel.

Now the absolute silence made her shiver.

A feeling that something was terribly amiss sent her suddenly dashing in the direction Andronicus had disappeared.

Crassus called her back, but she ignored him. She could hear the three men hurrying after her. She knew she was disobeying Andronicus's command to stay put, but something urged her on. No doubt the soldiers were more concerned about disobeying Andronicus than she was.

She stopped at the end of the village but could see no sign of Andronicus or Arius. The other men caught up with her, glancing around apprehensively. Like her, they grew uneasy at the two men's disappearance.

Noticing an open doorway, Tapat headed in that direction. She peeked her head in the opened door and almost gagged at the odor coming from inside.

She heard Arius's question to Andronicus. She stood frozen for an instant, horrified at what she had just heard. The callousness of what he was about to do horrified her almost as much as the thought of the act itself. Was Rome then so lacking in mercy or humanity? Was Andronicus?

Before Andronicus could answer Arius, she screamed a denial. Both men turned startled countenances her way. Andronicus's forehead drew together into a forbidding scowl.

"I told you to stay put!"

She ignored the comment and came farther into the hut. Andronicus put up a hand to stop her.

"Stay back! We don't know what kind of fever the woman has."

Tapat hesitated but a moment, then she hurried forward, intent on pushing her way through the two men, but their well-honed bodies were as solid as the mountains that surrounded Jerusalem.

Her pleading look meshed with Andronicus's fierce glare.

"Please," she begged. "Perhaps I can help."

Arius glanced from one to the other and frowned. "Tribune! We haven't the time," he cautioned.

Andronicus fixed the man with a steely look and Arius subsided. Andronicus then turned back to Tapat. His eyes warmed with compassion.

"We have to stay the night here anyway. What harm can come from trying to make her passing as easy as possible?" The fierce look was gone from his face, replaced by one of pity. "She cannot last, Tapat. And without nourishment, neither will the child."

The babe made a little mewling sound, and it was then that Tapat noticed the child. This time when she tried to pass, Andronicus allowed it.

She knelt by the woman's side, ignoring the strong smell. It was obvious she had been lying here unable to fend for herself for some time. Her body waste had soiled the sheets and blankets on her bed.

The child lay in a stupor beside her in the same condition. More than likely the mother's milk had dried up, but how long ago? How long could a babe survive without food? If something wasn't done soon, they would both die. Her lips settled into a hard, determined line. Not if she had anything to do with it!

Tapat turned to Andronicus. "I need water, lots of it. And a fire."

"Tapat..."

"Please!" she begged. "We have to try to help."

"My Lord..." Arius began heatedly but was interrupted by Crassus speaking from the doorway.

"I will get the water."

Crassus had stepped inside, but the others had remained outside. Tapat couldn't blame them. The smell was intense. She glanced at Crassus in approbation.

"Thank you."

Crassus awaited permission, his look fixed on Andronicus. Arius looked as though he was about to berate the young man, but Andronicus spoke before he could.

"Go."

Arius sighed heavily, his glance at Andronicus speaking his aggravation more readily than words. Andronicus ignored him, focusing instead on Tapat.

"What can I do?"

Tapat's heart swelled with gratitude. "I need clean bedding. Look through some of the other houses and see if there is any left that we can use. And I need some light."

Already the shadows had deepened with approaching night.

She glanced down at the baby and her heart nearly broke. "Perhaps the men can search the area and see if there might be a goat." It was doubtful, but she was desperate. She began an unending prayer to Elohim.

Andronicus turned to Arius. "You heard her. Take the men and see what you can find."

Arius snorted in disbelief. He gave Andronicus a look that told Tapat if they hadn't been friends, he would have let his commander know in no uncertain terms what he thought of him. Instead, he shoved past Andronicus and began barking orders at the men.

Tapat's distressed eyes met those of Andronicus. She was interfering in his command of his men and he was siding with her against his centurion.

"I'm sorry," she told him softly.

He didn't answer right away. He finally took a deep breath. "I'll go see about the bedding."

Crassus was just coming in the door with an urn of water when Andronicus left. He set the water to the side of the sleeping mat and looked at Tapat.

"I'll start the fire."

She thanked him with a look. He ducked back out the door, and she could hear him rummaging around trying to find wood to build a fire outside. She found herself wondering about the young man. How could he be so kind yet also be a soldier of Rome? The difference between him and Arius in regard to the woman and child was as wide as a chasm. Perhaps it had to do with time spent in Rome's army. Yet, Andronicus was unlike Arius, as well. Or was he? Would he have allowed the other man to kill the woman and child if not for her interference?

"I found a few things."

Andronicus's voice startled her out of her preoccupation, and she hurried to attend to the woman and child.

Crassus came back into the hut. "I have the fire going. What can I do now?"

Without looking at him, she gave instructions on how

to prepare a broth using a pot from the kitchen and some of their supplies. Before he did so, he lit the small lamp bowl filled with olive oil that Andronicus had found. The little bit of light cast eerie shadows dancing and gyrating across the walls.

Andronicus stood looking down at her as she wiped the woman's brow with a wet cloth. He had removed his helmet but retained his sword and armor. His curly dark hair clung wetly to his scalp. He was so handsome; in other circumstances, she would have been willing to stare at him forever.

"You know they will probably not survive, don't you?"

She looked away. "That is in Elohim's hands." She continued wiping the woman's face. "You can leave now. I need to undress the woman to clean her."

"Shall I attend to the child?"

Once again her heart swelled with gratitude. She didn't want to believe that Andronicus could be a ruthless Roman soldier, and it was at times like this that she felt she knew the *real* man—the one beneath all the Roman accoutrements.

"Thank you."

He gently lifted the lethargic baby and, ignoring the child's strong scent, cuddled the bundle close as he exited the house.

Tapat turned her attention to the woman. She was so thin that Tapat had no trouble lifting her body to remove her clothes. The woman couldn't have weighed more than a five-year-old child.

She then took the bedding Andronicus had provided and made a new bed on the other side of the room.

She searched the house for another garment that she could use but could find none. She wasn't surprised; from the look of things, this was a poor village, and most of the country's impoverished had only one garment to their name.

She poked her head out the door and found Crassus

stirring something in a clay pot over the fire. She glanced around for Andronicus but could see no sign of him nor of the others. Already the sun was setting behind the mountains in the distance. They were now in the approaching band of twilight. Darkness would soon make it impossible to see without some kind of light to illuminate the way.

"Crassus."

He glanced at her expectantly.

"Could you go to my horse, open the bag tied to its side and bring me the blue tunic you find there?"

He paused but then gave a jerk of his head in confirmation and hurried to do as she'd asked.

She went back inside and continued wiping down the woman's body. As she did so, the woman moaned softly.

Crassus came into the room, her blue tunic clutched in his hand. She hoped that Andronicus could forgive her for parting with the gift.

"Do you need help?" Crassus asked.

She shook her head. "No, not yet. I can manage to dress her but I will need your help to move her."

He looked at the woman, and Tapat was surprised by the pity she saw in his eyes. He gave Tapat a brief smile. "Just call me and I will come."

After she got the woman dressed, Crassus helped Tapat move her to the freshly made bed. He then took the soiled bedding outside. The scent in the room would take longer to eradicate, but it was less intense than before.

Crassus brought her a bowl of the broth, and Tapat took it, blowing to cool it. She had no idea whether the woman could swallow in her present condition, but she had to try. Although a person could go without food for a while, three days without water could kill a person. The small clay cup overturned beside the sleeping mat told its own story.

Tapat took a small spoonful of the broth and tried to feed it to the woman. Although some of it dribbled down the sides of her cheeks, Tapat was relieved to see that, even in her comatose state, her swallowing reflexes were normal. She fed her more, little bits at a time to keep her from choking.

Tapat glanced up when Andronicus came back into the house. He had rewrapped the child in clean cloths, not like the swaddling cloths of her people, but it would do. She gave him a smile and he returned it halfheartedly. She knew without asking that he was concerned at how she would handle things if the two died, knowing how recent her own grief was. Even she didn't understand the obsession that had overtaken her.

Andronicus noticed the blue tunic on the woman, and his eyes narrowed. He looked at Tapat for answer and she shrugged helplessly.

"There was no other."

He stared hard at her for several seconds before shaking his head in resignation. He seated himself at the table, still cuddling the babe. His face softened when he looked down at the child.

"Is it a boy or a girl?" Tapat asked him.

"A boy," he told her without looking up from the child's face.

"How is he doing?"

"Not well."

Those two little words said without inflection imparted more information than a brief recitation would have. Tapat's heart dropped to her toes.

A groaning from the mat caused Tapat's heart to quicken. She looked at her patient, relieved to see her slowly open her eyes, which were still glazed with fever.

She stared at Tapat uncomprehendingly.

"What is your name?" Tapat asked her softly in Aramaic, gently brushing the woman's hair out of her eyes.

"Martha," she croaked. Dawning comprehension widened her eyes. The ill woman tried to get up but was too weak to do more than lift her head and shoulders. She fell weakly back against the bed.

"My baby," she croaked. "Where is my baby?"

"He is here," she said, motioning for Andronicus to bring the child. He did so, and she gently laid the babe next to its mother. Martha was too weak to hold the baby on her own but was content to have him near. She looked down at her child and her eyes filled with tears. She knew without being told that the child hadn't long to live if something couldn't be done soon.

"How long have you been like this?" Tapat asked.

Martha looked up, and her glazed eyes darkened with memory. Her voice was no more than a whispered thread. "When the soldiers came, I was already in labor. I couldn't leave with the others."

Tapat was horrified. "Have you no family? What of your husband?"

"My husband was in Jerusalem for Passover." She paused, struggling for breath. "No one else was willing to stay.... The Romans..." Martha's voice grew fainter as she spoke.

Tapat was thankful that the woman couldn't see the two soldiers standing just outside the ring of light. She wanted to question Martha further but knew that she was barely hanging on to life as it was. Exhausted from her slight exertion, Martha closed her eyes.

"Can you manage to eat some broth if I feed you?"

"I will...try."

Tapat managed to get several spoons of broth into her before Martha once again slipped into unconsciousness.

She picked up the babe and cuddled him close. Large, lackadaisical brown eyes stared up at her. She could feel its bony frame through the coverings. How long had it been since he had had nourishment from his mother? Tears welled in her eyes, and she began to pray harder. Surely it could not be Elohim's will for her to have found them only to lose them.

Noise from outside alerted them seconds before Arius came into the house. He glanced at the woman and the child still held closely in Tapat's arms.

"Are they still alive?"

His disbelief was obvious. The other three men followed him into the house, decreasing the size of the room by half.

"They are alive," Andronicus told him. "Did you find a goat?"

He looked at Andronicus in wonder. "In fact, we did."

Tapat's mouth dropped open in amazement. "Praise Elohim!"

The look Arius gave her almost made her smile. She hadn't meant to take away his moment of triumph, but she knew where to give the true credit.

"I have no idea how you are going to manage to feed the child," he told her in irritation. "Nor do I know anything about milking a goat."

Neither did Tapat, but she knew now that the Lord had sent her to this place at this time for a specific purpose. If the two didn't survive, it would not be for lack of her trying.

"I can milk a goat," Crassus volunteered. His companions stared at him incredulously. All except Tapat. She was beginning to believe there was much more to the young man than was on the surface. She was also beginning to see Elohim's hand in all that was transpiring. It wasn't co-incidental that Crassus had been chosen to travel with them.

Crassus took a bowl and went outside to milk the goat. Now she had only to figure out how to get the milk into the babe.

Chapter 8

Andronicus thought of the stylus he used for writing buried among his supplies. With the sharp edge cut away, the reed tube could be used to slowly drop milk into the babe's mouth. He cut off the tip and washed out the dried ink that was inside.

He explained his idea to Tapat and then watched Tapat as she sat by the fire outside the hut cuddling the child close. She patiently dipped the pen into the bowl of milk, using her thumb to cover the open end. This allowed suction to hold the milk inside the straw tube. The babe suckled desperately for the sustenance as Tapat slowly released her thumb to allow the milk to be disbursed.

"I think it's going to work!" she told him, the smile in her voice reaching her eyes before it reached her lips.

He returned her smile with one of his own. It was good to see her face so full of joy again. She had gone from anxiety about the woman and her child to a calm acceptance that surprised him.

Andronicus, however, could tell that it took more energy to suckle than the child had in its already weakened condition. He was afraid that neither mother nor child was going to survive the night.

And if they did? What then? They couldn't remain here indefinitely, and he already knew that it was going to be a battle with Tapat to leave the two behind.

He glanced around the fire at his men.

Arius had taken the first watch and stood just outside the perimeter of the firelight. Tapat warily kept an eye on him, certain that at any moment he was about to dispatch the mother and child to the netherworld.

Celsus and Didius were sound asleep, their snores mingling with the snapping of the fire. Each man had his sword clutched against his chest.

Salvius kept nodding off and then jerking himself awake. He was trying hard to stay alert, but the day had been long and the heat oppressive. The heat sapped a man's energy more than anything. Even he was struggling to keep his eyes open.

Only Crassus seemed unaffected by the heat. He watched as the younger man got up from where he had been sitting and made his way to Tapat's side.

Andronicus's sleepiness instantly vanished. He tensed as Crassus squatted beside Tapat. He had noticed the young man studying Tapat throughout the day, and he hadn't liked it one little bit.

"I will see to the babe if you would like to check on the woman," he whispered.

Tapat looked surprised, but she was no more surprised by his concern for the little Jew than Andronicus was. Her face softened with a smile.

"Thank you. I would like that."

She handed the babe up to him and got to her feet. She watched a moment as he settled himself beside the fire and began the task of feeding the child. Satisfied that he was doing it properly, she went inside to check on Martha.

Andronicus got up, brushing the sand from his tunic, and followed her. He didn't miss the narrowed look Crassus threw his way before he ducked inside.

Tapat glanced up from where she was kneeling beside Martha. She was wiping a wet cloth across the woman's face and neck.

"She is so hot. I fed her some broth made with the willow bark you carry, but the fever is not abating."

Andronicus had learned of the willow bark medicine when he was in Germania. Now he never traveled without it. It had rarely failed to lower a fever, but he suspected in this case the woman's body was too weak from hunger to fight the fever off.

After many years on the battlefield, he could tell from the woman's breathing that she was closer to death than he had first imagined. He didn't want to upset Tapat further, so he kept the information to himself.

"You need to get some sleep," he told Tapat quietly, noting the dark circles under her eyes. The heat and the long hours were taking a toll on her.

She shook her head. "I cannot. I will be fine."

He wanted to argue but knew that it would be futile. "What can I do?" he asked instead.

She gave him a tired smile. "Nothing for the moment, but thank you for asking."

He hesitated, wanting to stay but knowing he should leave. Watching her care for the babe and the woman so tenderly had reminded him of his own mother. Tapat would make a wonderful wife and mother, and the more he was around her, the more he wanted to make that thought a reality. He had never wanted a woman so much in his life. But the barriers she had put in place held him firmly at arm's length. He needed to remove himself from the vicinity before he did something they would both regret.

"I'll be outside if you need me," he told her. She glanced up at him. When their gazes clashed, the tension in the room thickened. The attraction between them was growing with each passing day, but he knew it was impossible.

He made his way back to his place by the fire, his glance at Crassus suddenly caught by the look on the other man's face. If he didn't know better, he would think the soldier was warning him off. The look he returned gave a warning of its own and the younger man dropped his gaze.

It was some time before Tapat returned to the fire. She smiled down at Crassus, but he didn't immediately hand the child back to her.

"How is the mother?"

Tapat shook her head. "She is not well. I have done everything I know to do, but she is still burning with fever." She reached for the babe, but Crassus still didn't relinquish his possession.

"I can continue to feed him if you would like to get some sleep."

"Thank you, but you need to sleep yourself. I will sleep when the babe sleeps."

Crassus didn't argue further. He handed her the child but stayed seated beside Tapat. He glanced across at Andronicus, dropping his eyes quickly when Andronicus glared at him. Turning slightly away, he watched Tapat tending the baby while Andronicus watched him.

Andronicus could hear their whispered conversation.

"I have been wanting to ask you something," Crassus told Tapat. She cocked her head slightly, a lifted brow giving him permission to ask.

"Are you…" He lowered his voice further until Andronicus could barely catch the next part of his question. "Are you a Christian?"

* * *

Tapat looked up, startled, the color leaching from her face. The question was so unexpected, it took her a moment to get her thoughts together. She glanced across at Andronicus, who had sat up abruptly. He shook his head in warning.

She stared at Crassus for several long seconds. Fear tried to muzzle her mouth, but she could no more deny her Lord than she could stop her heart from beating.

"I mean you no harm!" he rushed to reassure her.

"Why do you ask me such a question?" she enquired, postponing giving him a direct answer. She could see Andronicus watching them intently. There was no doubt that if Crassus meant her harm, Andronicus would step in to protect her.

"You remind me of someone," Crassus told her.

Tapat could feel her heart suddenly pounding with trepidation. She wasn't certain where this conversation was going.

"She is a Christian?" she asked reluctantly.

Crassus nodded, drawing his knees up to his chest and placing his chin on them. "The song you were singing to the babe, I have heard her sing it."

She hadn't been aware of what she was singing at the time, but the words came back to her now. It was a special psalm of King David the believers often sang during worship on the Lord's Day. The words always brought peace to her heart, and she had hoped they would soothe the ailing infant.

"Where did you hear her sing it?"

He picked up another stick and threw it onto the fire. Tapat had the feeling it was as much to avoid looking at her as to keep the fire going. He delayed answering so long, she was afraid he wasn't going to. Finally, he looked at her almost apologetically.

"She is a slave in my father's household. She often sings it while working in the garden."

Something in his voice made her glance at him suspiciously. It was clear that his feelings were involved in some way. Several thoughts caromed through her mind, not all of them pleasant. If the girl was a slave, had Crassus taken advantage of his position as her master? The thought chilled her despite the hot night air blowing against her skin.

"You are in love with her." It was more a statement than a question.

He nodded and, against her will, her eyes were drawn across the way to Andronicus. Every time she looked into his eyes, her own resolve to hold herself aloof wavered. In his eyes she could see the hope for a future together that she knew could not be. She dragged her gaze back to Crassus.

"Your father is all right with her being a Christian?" she asked, knowing that Rome had never been tolerant of those who followed the Way.

"He doesn't know."

Again, his voice suggested more than the words he said. She didn't know how to answer that heartrending statement.

"And does she love you?"

His look was so doleful, Tapat's own heart went out to him.

"She is afraid of me. She sees me as nothing but a master."

Tapat's empathy for the unknown young woman grew. Did she struggle day after day with the desire to stay in Elohim's will when her heart yearned for something much different? Were her feelings being torn apart with the daily struggle to stay true to her vows while loving a man who was a heathen?

"Are you certain that is how she sees you?"

"How else?" he growled. "She runs every time she sees me coming!" He looked at Tapat helplessly. "I know it is your God that makes her different, that makes her special. I want to understand, but how can I when she won't even talk to me?"

Tapat was impressed that Crassus hadn't used his position of authority to force the woman to his will. He was very much like Andronicus that way, and she felt a growing sympathy for him.

She looked across at Andronicus and could tell that he had heard the entire conversation. He was waiting to hear how she answered, his dark eyes glittering with empathy, but she had no idea how to counsel the young man. She was as confused as he.

She focused her attention on the babe to give herself time to think. The child had stopped moving and his eyes were closed. Tapat panicked, all other thoughts fleeing. She quickly felt for a pulse against the boy's tiny neck, reassured when she felt it beating weakly against her searching fingers. He had fallen asleep, his little stomach, if not full, at least replete for the time being.

Her breath rushed out in a sigh of relief.

"He is well?" Crassus asked in concern.

Tapat smiled reassuringly. "He is asleep."

Crassus moved restlessly, and she could sense that he wanted to continue their conversation but was uncertain how to begin.

"Tell me of this girl," she encouraged. "What is her name?"

She smiled at his look of relief.

"Her name is Lydia."

Tapat allowed him to talk, answering his questions unreservedly about her faith and more reservedly when it came to a discourse of love. He was not satisfied with her answers, his frustration evident as he tried to understand how a woman could love a God over a man.

Her eyes grew heavier and she struggled to remain

awake. She had no idea when Andronicus had risen from his position across from her, but suddenly he was at her side.

"Come," he commanded. "I have prepared a place for you to sleep in the hut."

Crassus glanced contritely from one to the other. "My apologies, my liege. I should have seen that she was tired."

Tapat shook her head. "No, I am fine. The babe will need to be fed again soon."

Andronicus ignored her. Taking the child from her arms, he handed him to Crassus and then lifted Tapat to her feet.

"The babe will sleep for some time. I will awaken you when he stirs."

She tried to pull her arm free from his hold, but he was unyielding. She stopped struggling, glaring up at him. "Do you give me your word?"

He knew what she was afraid of, had been afraid of ever since she had heard Arius threaten to take the two lives. Instead of being angry, his features softened. "Trust me," he demanded softly.

Their gazes collided and she knew that he was talking about so much more than this moment in time. She took a deep breath, dropping her eyes to the ground. She nodded in consent. She had no choice for the time being.

Crassus looked from one to the other, a dawning look of understanding creasing his rugged features. Tapat colored hotly at his knowing look.

Now that the responsibility of the child was taken from her, Tapat could no longer stave off the exhaustion that had been threatening to claim her for the past several hours. She staggered and Andronicus swept her up into his arms. She couldn't bring herself to look him in the face until he gently laid her on a mat across from Martha.

He knelt by her side, gently pushing the hair from her face. No words were exchanged, but Tapat felt the subtle change in their relationship. Had Crassus's story of Lydia caused him to give more thought to their own situation?

Crassus came into the hut and laid the child next to Tapat. He glanced from Andronicus to Tapat and then quickly left.

Andronicus got to his feet. "I will see you when you awaken."

Feeling more confident with the child lying next to her, Tapat managed a smile.

When Andronicus left, all the energy of the room seemed to leave with him.

Yawning, Tapat only had time to see that Martha was still breathing before she closed her eyes and instantly slept.

Chapter 9

When Tapat opened her eyes again, daylight was streaming in the open door and the babe was gone.

Bolting upright, she glanced over and noticed the mat across from her was empty, as well. Small prickles of apprehension shivered through her. Heart pounding, she quickly got to her feet and rushed outside, blinking against the already bright sunlight.

Crassus was sitting cross-legged on a wooden bench propped against the house and carefully feeding the babe with the modified stylus. Tapat slowly released the breath she didn't even know she had been holding.

He glanced up when she approached but quickly dropped his eyes to the suckling child. She hadn't missed the concern in his sad look, and she almost choked on the knot climbing its way up her throat. She quickly glanced around the area for some sign of Martha.

"You were sleeping so soundly, you didn't hear the babe

crying," he told her uneasily. "We thought it best to let you get more sleep."

"Where's Martha?"

Andronicus answered her. He came and placed a hand on her shoulder. "I'm sorry, Tapat. The woman died during the night."

Her face registered her shock and suspicion. Her bottom lip began to quiver, and he sighed.

"It's not what you think," he told her quietly, pulling her into his arms. "When I went to check on you and the babe, I found that the woman had stopped breathing. I removed her, trying not to wake you, and Celsus saw to her burial outside the village."

She wondered how she could have slept so deeply that nothing of those events had aroused her. She had failed Martha.

The woman, Andronicus had said. As though she were some unimportant piece of flotsam. As though she were not a beloved child of Elohim. She pushed out of his arms, filled with a sudden, inconceivable rage.

"Her name was Martha!" she spat furiously, tears suddenly blurring her vision. Andronicus lifted his brows in surprise at her vehemence. He frowned, trying to understand what was happening to her when she didn't fully understand it herself. Once the tears started, there was no end.

She fought Andronicus as he tried to hold her once again, but he easily overcame her resistance. He held her quietly and allowed her grief to expend itself.

It horrified her that Martha had died alone with no one there to comfort her. It was something she had always feared for herself—dying alone with no one to even remember her name. It was why she was so determined to be there for her mother, to make certain that she didn't die alone. And yet she had. Although Tapat had continued to care for her by bringing her food and supplies, she could not enter the Valley of Lepers and her mother had indeed died alone. In one of the caves.

It was hard to swallow past the knot in her throat. She felt numb, as though she had taken a massive dose of mandragora. But at least her mother had known of Jesus, the Christ. So in reality, she hadn't really died alone because He promised to be with them always. It was that thought, more than anything, that had brought her the most comfort.

Did Martha know of Christ? Were the people in this village believers? The rudely carved cross that she had found in Martha's house gave her hope that this might be so.

Andronicus finally allowed her to leave the comforting circle of his arms once her tears were spent. He studied her face closely, and she set her chin resolutely.

"Are you all right?" he asked.

"I am fine."

She noticed Didius attaching the goat's lead to their supply horse. The other horses were saddled and ready, as well. She turned to Andronicus in surprise.

"Are we leaving?"

He nodded. "We have a long way to go yet."

"But the babe…"

"We have no choice. We can't stay here."

He handed Tapat a plate with a piece of bread, some cheese and dates.

"Go ahead and eat. The others have already done so."

Celsus and Salvius had finished scouring through the other huts for tools or other items that might help them on their journey. Salvius had tried to give her a tunic he had found in one of the houses, but Tapat had adamantly refused despite the fact that hers was so threadbare it would probably not last another season. It bothered her to take things that weren't rightfully hers; the soldiers, however, appeared to have no such scruples. She supposed that looting was just another part of what went into being a soldier.

Despite her lack of appetite, she carefully broke her bread into little pieces, fully aware of the soldiers' impatience to be gone, but by taking as much time as possible to eat, it would give Crassus more time to feed the babe. The slower she ate, the more time the child had to suckle. It was a time-consuming operation, feeding one dropperful of milk at a time. She was thankful to the young soldier for helping her.

Arius stood impatiently near the horses, his arms crossed over his chest. He watched her choke down one piece of bread at a time as she warily kept an eye on him. She had the distinct feeling that he knew she was deliberately delaying them. She gave him a guarded look, which only made him smile wryly in return.

Although she had overheard him talk of killing Martha and the babe, she couldn't make herself believe that he would have really done so, nor could she imagine Andronicus standing aside and allowing it. And despite herself, she liked Arius. He reminded her very much of Andronicus. She instinctively felt that she could trust him.

When the babe finally fell asleep again, Tapat set her plate aside, popped the last piece of bread in her mouth and rose to retrieve him from Crassus.

Seeing that she had finished, the soldiers quickly moved to mount the horses, but Tapat needed to do one more thing first. She hugged the babe close and hesitantly approached Andronicus.

"Please take me to where Martha is buried."

He frowned in objection. "We haven't time."

"Please," she begged him, ignoring the frowns of the other men. She also pleaded with her eyes, begged him, and his eyes darkened from their normal cinnamon color until she could see her own reflection.

He sighed in resignation and, shaking his head at what

he considered her folly, he took her to where Celsus had buried the body.

Tapat stared forlornly at the freshly turned dirt. She knelt by the grave, brushing her hand across the sun-warmed surface. By Jewish law she had just made herself unclean, but she didn't care. Her heart broke for the woman who had fought to keep her child alive while she was herself dying. Such devotion, such love, deserved respect.

She bowed her head and soundlessly mouthed a prayer as Andronicus shifted impatiently beside her. When she had finished, she stared at the grave and a lone tear wound its way down her cheek. She sniffed it back, determined not to give Andronicus cause to think her some emotional female who would be a burden to him and the men.

"I promise you," she whispered to the grave, "I will see that your son has a home. I will teach him about Jesus, and, Elohim willing, one day you will see him again."

"We should give him a name," Crassus spoke gruffly from behind her. So intent had she been on her prayers, she hadn't even heard him join them. "We can't keep calling him 'the babe.'"

He was right, of course. Crassus's concern for the child was touching, especially knowing the Roman law of casting a babe aside if there was something wrong with the child or if it wasn't wanted.

Tapat gazed lovingly into the infant's face. This child was neither imperfect nor unwanted—that much was obvious by his mother's devotion.

"I wonder what Martha named him?" she queried softly. Jews gave much thought to the naming of their children. It was not something to be taken lightly.

Andronicus came to stand beside her. He gently stroked a finger down the child's soft cheek. Tapat noticed that his handsome face was wreathed with unease.

"You don't think he will survive, do you?" Tapat asked, worrying her bottom lip with her teeth.

Andronicus shrugged. "He has shown himself to be a strong child. He is still very weak, but I would not doubt his will to survive."

His words brought Tapat hope. In just the short time she had been caring for the child, she had come to love him. Who wouldn't?

Andronicus smiled. "Why don't *you* give him a name?"

"I agree," Crassus grinned. "Who better?"

Tapat looked from one to the other. It was a daunting prospect. Because the babe was older than eight days, he would have been circumcised and given a name of his parents' choosing, either a family name or something that would have explained his birth. If only she had thought to ask Martha before the sickness claimed her life.

They were right, though. A child needed a name. She would use Andronicus's words to give him a name and a designation. She chose one in Hebrew.

"I will call him Hazaq," she told them, cuddling the babe close, "because he is strong. And he *will* survive." She glared at each man in turn, her fierce, uncompromising look daring them to disagree. They wisely remained silent.

All except Arius, who had just arrived at the burial site. He gave a soft snort and turned to Andronicus. "Tribune," he called, "the day is only going to get hotter."

Andronicus took Tapat's arm and moved her toward the horses. She looked over her shoulder, the lone grave filling her with sadness. Would the people of this village ever return? Would Martha's husband live through the coming siege and wonder what had become of his family? Or would the huts remain empty for years to come, slowly being eradicated by the sands of time? It made her heart heavy just thinking about it.

Andronicus gave Hazaq to Crassus and lifted Tapat into

the saddle, then handed her the sleeping babe. Tapat ignored his searching look and carefully arranged the blanket over Hazaq to protect him from the hot Palestinian sun. She knew it was probably just her hopeful imagination, but he seemed to be much stronger today.

Holding Hazaq in her arms, Tapat had to grip the horse with her thighs to keep from falling off. Andronicus's look of sympathy told her that he was aware of her predicament but that there was nothing else to be done. She settled back to endure the long ride.

Andronicus knew that at the end of the day, Tapat's legs were going to hurt something fierce. He deliberately pulled back, well aware that his men didn't like the slower pace.

He had hoped to make it to Pella in two or three days, but it now looked as if it would take much longer. They would need to stop periodically to allow Tapat to feed the babe. It was something he hadn't counted on, but the Fates had dealt him a different hand. Or was it Tapat's God who had done so? At least she seemed to think so.

They were fortunate to have found the village in which to spend the past evening; Tapat had used the word *blessed*. He doubted they would be so fortunate again this coming night. He almost sent up a prayer to Tapat's Jewish God but then rebuked himself sternly. It was easier to believe in the capricious Fates than to believe in a God who would allow His Son to die mercilessly on a wretched cross. That form of punishment was used only for the most nefarious of crimes. Surely a true god would never allow his son to die in such a despicable way.

Arius led the way, followed by Andronicus leading Tapat's horse. Crassus was behind her, with the others bringing up the rear.

The men were too well trained to complain about the dawdling pace. Only Crassus seemed content to plod along.

Periodically he would push his horse to a faster pace to catch up with Tapat and ask after her welfare. His constant attention was becoming increasingly annoying to Andronicus.

Traveling through the hot desert countryside was a tedious business. Sweat poured from under his metal helmet and armor chest piece, yet he knew better than to travel without the protection that had helped to keep him alive so many times in the past.

They might be traveling in the desert, but the threat of attack was just as likely as when traveling through the tree-studded hills of Germania. The desert people knew their territory and were adept at keeping hidden among the rocks and crags. Those pockets of resistance still were scattered throughout the countryside and bent on eliminating as many of Rome's forces as they could.

They were now making their way through an area known for cutthroats and bandits. Many people had lost their lives on this treacherous pathway, Jew and Roman alike.

Suddenly his soldier's instinct went on alert. He could see by the stiffening postures of his men that they had the same reaction.

He glanced back at Tapat and found Crassus close beside her, his eyes seeking any hidden enemies that might be lurking about. For once, Andronicus was glad to see the other man's protective attitude.

Knowing the danger, Andronicus didn't object when Arius picked up their pace. He dropped back to take Hazaq from Tapat so that she could hold on to her horse with both hands. She reluctantly handed the child over. Having ridden for years, Andronicus had no problem holding on to Hazaq and his reins at the same time.

The eerie silence as they traveled along after the men's earlier chatter was unnerving. Time seemed to drag. Anxiety mounted.

They finally made it through the area without mishap and, after traveling several more miles, the ease of tension among them was palpable. He returned the sleeping babe to Tapat, sensing her unease at having the child gone from her arms. She immediately hugged him close, her smile of appreciation warming Andronicus as effectively as the desert sun.

Andronicus waited until they were farther beyond the Jericho Valley before calling a halt in an area that sported a few trees that could be used to shade them while they rested. Hazaq had awoken earlier and was making a racket that let them know he wanted sustenance and he wanted it *now*. It was reassuring that the child could cry with such vigor.

They climbed from their horses, but Tapat remained seated until Crassus went to her and took Hazaq. Andronicus reached her side just as her feet touched the sand. She would have crumpled to the ground if he hadn't been there to catch her.

"Give your legs a moment to adjust," he warned.

She clung to him a few seconds until her legs grew steadier, then pushed herself out of his hold and reached for the babe. Each time Andronicus held her, he was more reluctant to release her. Their time together grew shorter the farther north they went.

It took a few moments for Crassus to get the goat to calm down enough for him to milk it, but he finally presented Tapat with a bowl of the warm liquid.

She settled herself on a boulder in the shade of a tamarack tree and began the slow ritual of feeding the babe. He hungrily suckled on the stylus and Tapat smiled, making Andronicus's heart swell with emotion. When her face was lit with such love, she was beautiful to him.

He went and sat on the boulder with her. The others sought sources of shade as well, pulling their water flasks from their saddles and refreshing themselves as best they could with the warm liquid.

Andronicus held his goatskin up for Tapat to take a drink because her arms were already burdened with feeding Hazaq. She drank thirstily, pulling back when her thirst was quenched.

Water dribbled down her chin. Smiling, Andronicus wiped it away with his thumb. Their eyes met, and he could feel the tension increase as it always did whenever they were this close.

"Thank you," she murmured, turning her attention back to Hazaq.

He nodded, lifting the skin and quickly satisfying his own thirst. He only wished his thirst for her was as easily quenched.

He could tell he was making Tapat nervous, so instead of watching her, he studied the landscape around him. Heat shimmered from the surface of the hot sand, making the terrain move in waves.

The area was so desolate that he wondered again why these Jews fought so fiercely to keep such a land. In truth, it was something the Romans had never been able to understand and thereby often misjudged the people's willingness to fight and die.

When Hazaq was once again replete, he stopped sucking and smiled around the straw still in his mouth.

"He's smiling," Tapat crooned and began cooing to him. If she wasn't in love with the child before, he could tell she was a lost cause now. He shook his head wryly. Her God alone knew how this whole affair was going to end. Did Tapat have any idea of what it would be like to care for a child on her own?

Tapat interrupted his thoughts by handing Hazaq to him. His heart took a startled leap, and he swallowed an unfamiliar panic. Tapat grinned.

"He won't bite. I need to get some changing rags."

Andronicus slowly rearranged the child in his arms, wrinkling his nose at the stench arising from him. How could one little babe be responsible for such an overwhelming, disgusting odor? When Hazaq smiled at him, Andronicus felt a strange warmth spread through him. Those dark eyes staring up at him reminded him so much of Tapat's.

Tapat went to her horse and pulled some cloths from the supplies the soldiers had confiscated from the village. Coming back, she spread a blanket on the sand. Taking the child from him, she laid him on it and began unwrapping the soiled swaddling cloths.

She talked to the child as though he could understand every word she said. She switched periodically from Aramaic to Greek, making it hard to follow her rambling conversation. He shook his head. He would never understand women and the way they turned into a puddle of mush whenever a babe was in the vicinity.

After she had rewrapped the child to her satisfaction, she placed the soiled garments in a leather bag to be washed later. In his opinion, she could just as easily throw them away and get new ones from the stockpile they had pilfered from the village.

He watched her interacting with Hazaq and once again felt an overwhelming tenderness fill him.

"How old do you think he is?" he asked.

She shrugged. "I'm not certain, but I would guess at least three months."

Arius came over. As he glanced at the babe, Andronicus was certain he saw a softening of his features.

"It is time we move on, my liege."

Andronicus agreed. He helped Tapat to her feet.

After they had remounted and traveled several more miles, Andronicus noticed a brown haze in the distance.

He paused, studying the rapidly approaching cloud. Arius noticed it as well and held a hand up for their troop to stop.

He turned to Andronicus, his eyes wide in consternation. "It's a sandstorm."

Their eyes met in understanding. They needed to find shelter and find it fast. In the babe's weakened condition, he would not survive the suffocating sand that would bear down upon them, infiltrating every nook and cranny, including one's nose and throat.

Chapter 10

Tapat realized that they were in a terrible predicament when she saw the worried look on the men's faces. She followed their gazes and saw the rapidly approaching sandstorm in the distance. Having lived in Judea all her life, she knew the danger they were in. What looked to be a great distance away would be upon them in minutes.

During a *sharav* summer, sandstorms were frequent and often violent. This had been one of those years.

"The only chance we have is to make it to the other side of that hill," Arius yelled, pointing just ahead of them as the winds that preceded the storm began to increase.

Tapat measured the distance to the hill he was indicating and knew they would never make it, not at the pace they were traveling.

Andronicus glanced from the storm to the hill. His mouth set in a grim line. He held out the reins of Tapat's horse. "Crassus, take the horse!" he commanded.

Crassus quickly pushed his horse ahead of Tapat and

took the lines being held out to him. Andronicus then moved his horse alongside Tapat.

"Hold on to the babe!" he told her.

Tapat only had time to tighten her grip on Hazaq before Andronicus reached over and pulled her off her horse and across his lap. When he was assured that she was firmly seated, he looked sternly at the others.

"You know what to do."

They nodded, and Andronicus twisted his horse around and dug his heels into the animal's side. His sinewy arm wrapped around her waist was the only thing that kept her from sliding to the dirt as they leaped forward.

"Adeo!"

At his command to go, they took off in a bone-wrenching gallop that nearly shook Tapat's teeth from her head. The pounding pace wakened the babe, who began to cry lustily, letting them know in no uncertain terms that he was not at all pleased. She tried to keep him from being jarred by the brutal pace, but, no matter how tightly she held him, the jostling was severe. She could hear the others galloping close behind them and could see Arius just ahead.

When they reached the embankment, Andronicus spurred his horse up, its hooves slipping and sliding against the rock outcropping as it plunged its way to the top and finally over the other side. They made it to the bottom of the hill just as the first of the sand began stinging their skin.

Before Tapat could even think what to do, Crassus was at their side reaching for Hazaq. Realizing just how much she had come to trust the young man, Tapat quickly handed him over.

Andronicus leaped from the horse, pulling Tapat into his arms and hurrying her to where Crassus had found a sizable depression in the hillside.

He pushed her into the cleft and Crassus handed her the screaming babe. As Tapat tried to soothe Hazaq, Andronicus tore off his cloak and dropped it over them, plunging them into sudden darkness. He then covered them both with his body to more fully protect them from the wind and flying sand.

In the suffocating darkness, Tapat could hear the wind increase in tempo. Buried beneath the cape and Andronicus's body, she heard the sounds of the other men and the horses as though from a distance. She began a prayer for their safety, especially for little Hazaq, who was still weak.

The darkness increased and the wind and sand seemed to lessen when the soldiers managed to finally cover them all with a goatskin tent. They struggled to secure the tent against the now gusting winds. She heard Andronicus warn them to hang on tightly to the corners of the skin to keep the wind from whipping it away.

Andronicus carefully uncovered Tapat to avoid dusting her with the sand that had accumulated on his cloak. Tapat sucked in a breath, relieved to be free from the cloistered space, although the tent didn't offer much more with all of them huddled close together. She could barely see Andronicus in the dim light.

"Are you all right?" he asked.

Between the sound of the sandstorm outside and the screaming child inside, Tapat could barely hear him.

She raised her voice above the din. "I'm well."

He pulled her to him, wrapping his arms around her to make room for the others crowded into the small makeshift structure.

Tapat tried to soothe Hazaq, bouncing him gently in her arms. She stuck a finger in his mouth and he quieted, content to suck on the imaginary food source. She didn't know how long it would continue to pacify him, but the relief from his screaming lessened her nervous tension.

As the storm continued, Tapat lost track of time. The air

in their structure turned stifling. She could feel the perspiration streaming down her face and back.

Hazaq had given up on sucking her finger long ago, and his tormented screams twisted her insides. No matter what she tried, nothing could calm the child. If the heat was unbearable for her, what must it be like for him? It was long past the time when he normally would have fed. She could only hope that when the storm subsided the goat would not have wandered away nor have been buried by the flying sand.

Talk was minimal. The clamor from without and within precluded having any kind of rational conversation.

The air grew rank from seven sweaty bodies that hadn't seen a bath in several days. When the babe added his aroma to the mix, the atmosphere grew stifling.

Just when Tapat thought she could stand it no longer, the wind began to abate. She sensed more than heard the other men as they relaxed from battling the elements.

Andronicus drew his cape over her again. "Stay covered," he told her. "The wind has slowed but the sand is still blowing. Wait until we see if it is safe."

She could hear the cover being thrown back and the men scrambling to their feet. She pulled the cloak away from her face and took a deep breath, but she kept Hazaq covered until the stinging sand subsided. His little fists fought against the stifling cover, his voice becoming hoarse from screaming.

She could see that both the goat and the horses had been hobbled to keep them from running away. They were a pitiful sight, heads hanging to the ground and covered with a thick coating of sand.

Crassus immediately went to work to get some milk from the goat while the others checked over the horses and supplies. He turned his back to the wind to keep the sand from entering the bowl, and she once again appreciated his concern for Hazaq.

The sand finally quit blowing when the wind settled down to a gentle, hot breeze.

She uncovered Hazaq and noticed that his face was red from heat and crying. His cries had become hoarse little croaks. She could only pray that he had grown strong enough in the past two days to withstand the afflictions they were putting him through. If only they could have remained in the village for a few more days.

Andronicus brought the water flask to her and helped her get a drink. "Spit out the first mouthful," he warned, and she could see the sense in the command when she felt the grit in her mouth.

She did as he suggested and then he upturned the flask further to give her better access to swallow. The water was tepid but still soothing to a throat parched from heat and sand.

Crassus brought her the milk and stylus, settling himself beside her to help if necessary.

Andronicus watched Tapat and Crassus without appearing to do so. Crassus's concern over the child had surprised him. He wasn't certain if it was the child who drew him or Tapat. They conversed quietly. At times Tapat's face became animated with an excitement he had rarely seen. She and Crassus seemed to have a lot to talk about. The thought left him feeling more than a little disgruntled.

The storm had put them even further behind on time. He had hoped to be closer to the Jordan River tonight, but at the slow pace they were setting, that wasn't going to happen. The closer they were to Perea and away from Judea, the happier he would be. They were still too close to wandering bandit territory for him to feel comfortable, and Perea was much more tolerant of Rome than Judea.

Now, after the two-hour storm, they had to wait for the babe to feed.

Andronicus walked over and leaned on the rock face of the hill beside Tapat.

Crassus met his look, reading Andronicus's lifted brow for what it was. He shifted uneasily and rose quickly to his feet.

"I have things to attend to," he told Tapat. "Let me know when you are ready to go and I will help you with the babe." His glance bounced off Andronicus before he quickly walked away.

Tapat was struggling to keep up with the babe's thirst and hunger.

"If I had to stay under that tent one more minute, I think my screaming would have joined with Hazaq's," she told him with a faint smile that warned him just how close to telling the truth she was. "How could you and your men remain so calm?"

He gave a gentle snort, his glance searching out each of his men. They quietly and skillfully went about their work. If their nerves had been frayed by the squalling infant, they gave no sign. Regardless of the unexpected delays and surprises, they remained calm and focused. He felt a fierce pride in them and knew he had chosen well for this trip.

"You have never been near a battle, have you?" he asked her.

She shook her head, looking at him quizzically.

His voice deepened at best-forgotten reminiscences. "When you are in battle, bodies crush in on you from all sides. The sound of metal on metal, scream on scream, battle call on battle call echoes all around until you cannot hear your heart pounding in your ears." He glanced down when she placed her hand sympathetically on his, and he felt a tremor ripple through his body. He almost forgot what he had been about to say.

"You learn to ignore anything around you until you no longer hear the sounds," he finally finished. "All you hear is the voice inside your head trying to keep you alive."

She swallowed hard at his description, her features wreathed with concern. He shook his head to free it of the encroaching memories. He hadn't meant to sound so morbid. It was a way of life he had lived with for years.

Perhaps that's what drew him so much toward Tapat. Her dark eyes were like calm, peaceful pools that he yearned to immerse himself in.

"These men have seen many battles," he admitted, wondering if Crassus saw the same thing in Tapat.

Tapat glanced at each man with growing respect.

Arius joined them. "What now? The hour grows late. Do we stay here or move on?"

Andronicus glanced down at the sleeping infant. More than likely it was from sheer exhaustion instead of satiation. He would likely wake in a short time wanting more sustenance. He didn't like the idea of staying here, but neither did he think it would be wise to leave. At least here they had some protection by the craggy hill.

"Let's make camp here for the night. I think we could all use the rest, including the animals."

Arius glanced briefly at Tapat. When his eyes met Andronicus's, they held a warning. *"Periculum in mora."*

Andronicus frowned at the reminder that it was dangerous to delay. He didn't need to be told that; he was well aware of the fact. And despite their many years of friendship, he was not about to have his orders questioned.

"Dixi!"

Arius straightened at the reminder of Andronicus's authority. He gave a brief nod. *"Libet."*

Andronicus watched him walk away and give orders to the men. They quickly turned from packing supplies to making camp instead.

The tent normally used for his own personal use would be set up for Tapat and the babe instead. He had no problem with sleeping under the starry skies. It gave him a sense of freedom and camaraderie with his men that was lacking in the more formal setting when he was separated by his own sleeping quarters.

He noticed that Tapat looked weary. Crassus brought her more linen cloths to change Hazaq when he awoke, and she thanked him with a tired smile.

While the others went about setting up camp, Andronicus gathered dry brush and sticks for a fire. Although the fire wasn't needed for warmth nor for making a meal, it was warranted in case of predators.

Hazaq awoke again after a few hours and Tapat began the feeding ritual. Andronicus settled next to her, watching as the babe hungrily suckled down the milk. His large brown eyes stared up at Andronicus with absolute trust, and the feelings that suddenly swarmed through Andronicus made him understand Tapat's passionate desire to protect the child.

"I told you he was strong," he told her, unaware of the pride in his own voice. He tickled the babe under his chin and was rewarded with a smile.

Tapat's eyes met his and the warmth he saw in them melted his insides, his heart rate rising until it felt as if it would burst from his chest. He was once again reminded of how much power this woman seemed to hold over him. The rapid rise and fall of her chest told him that she was as much affected as he. When the pupils of her eyes softened and dilated, he knew he needed to quickly put some distance between them.

Dragging his gaze away, he got to his feet and went to arrange for the coming watches, forcing himself not to look back.

Arius stood on the perimeter of the camp staring outward, hands fisted on his waist. Andronicus joined him.

"Is something bothering you?"

Arius shrugged, his eyes narrowing. "Just a feeling."

Andronicus truly became concerned. Arius's *feelings* had saved his life more than once.

"What do you sense?" Andronicus asked, now studying the terrain more intensely.

"Something hidden," he said. "Some hidden malice that we cannot see."

At the other man's prophetic voice, Andronicus searched for Tapat's location to make certain she was where he had left her. She was calmly feeding the babe while the men reclined on their blankets and discussed the day's storm. Crassus had once again made his way to Tapat's side, and they were again in deep discussion. Everything seemed perfectly normal.

The encroaching night brought out the nocturnal creatures. Crickets chirped in the distance. He could hear an owl hoot not far away, and in the far distance he could hear the roar of a lion.

When the crickets suddenly stopped chirping, Andronicus straightened and Arius visibly tensed, pulling his sword from its scabbard.

Andronicus only had time to pull his own sword and yell, "To arms!" before a group of men came out of seemingly thin air and attacked.

Tapat jerked her head up at Andronicus's yell. Crassus was on his feet in an instant, his sword out and primed for battle. He planted his feet firmly in front of her, intent on defending her and the baby if the battle moved this way.

Chaos broke out all around. She hugged Hazaq close, her eyes widening in terror as a group of men swarmed the camp, their yells sounding loud amid the clanging of sword on sword.

She could see Andronicus slashing and swinging his sword, Arius at his side doing the same. They were hopelessly outnumbered. She placed a hand urgently on Crassus's leg.

"Go, Crassus! Go and help them!"

He glanced down at her, his eyes glittering. "My orders…"

"Go," she interrupted. "They will not harm me."

He helplessly glanced back at where the fighting was fiercest. Celsus dropped to one knee as two men hacked away at him. Didius was warding off three others, his sword flashing left and right in a way only a soldier of Rome could accomplish.

Crassus looked down at Tapat again, his eyes full of anguish.

"Go," Tapat whispered, and he turned and leaped across the distance to join the fight.

She sat frozen, unable to do anything except watch as the battle played out around her.

Huddled against the hill, no one took notice of her or Hazaq. The child's screams couldn't be heard above the cacophony. She cuddled him close, but the noise raging around him frightened him and he refused to be comforted. It didn't help that her own fear was communicating itself to him, as well.

The Romans fought ferociously yet with great skill, their minds completely on the combat at hand.

She saw men fall to the ground, their lifeless eyes staring upward; she realized they were her countrymen. As yet, all the Romans were still on their feet. They fought with a skill and precision she had never seen before and hoped never to again. Their unified attack and defense allowed them to be seemingly in two places at a time. For the first time, she understood what Andronicus had meant about their concentration.

Her feelings were ambivalent. She understood all too well the Jews' desire to be free from Roman oppression, but she also knew that she could never ask Elohim to intercede in something that would bring about the death of Andronicus, nor his men, who she had come to like and admire.

After several Jews fell to their deaths, the others began to disband and run away.

One man turned to escape over the hill and noticed her and Hazaq. His eyes took on a glittering hue and she realized that he believed her to be the consort of one of the soldiers. He rushed at her, yelling wildly.

Tapat pulled Hazaq beneath her and covered him with her body. At least when he struck her, the babe would be protected.

She glanced over her shoulder, her face settling into lines of resolution.

"Lord Jesus," she whispered, "protect Hazaq and receive my spirit."

She heard Crassus yell and saw him running toward them. Time seemed to slow as both men converged on her location almost simultaneously. The Jew raised his sword to strike, but Crassus leaped across the space, his body twisting in midair as he turned his sword up to deflect the blow.

Sword clanged against sword and Crassus landed on his back, sliding several feet across the ground. He didn't have time to ready himself before the Jew slashed his sword down, catching Crassus across the chest and forearm. Crassus didn't move again.

The Jew suddenly jerked forward, head thrown backward, eyes wide, mouth open. He crumpled to the ground, a Roman *pilum* protruding from his back.

Staring in horror, Tapat glanced up to see Andronicus, feet spread apart, facing in their direction, arm still poised from throwing the spear and the fury of battle flashing in his dark eyes. The remaining Jews scrambled away to safety. Arius and the others started to give chase, but Andronicus's barked command stopped them in their tracks.

Arius stood immobile, his chest heaving and his bloody sword still in hand ready to meet any further attack, as the others rushed to Crassus's side.

Tapat wanted to go to him as well but she was hindered by the still screaming Hazaq.

Crassus lay unmoving, blood oozing onto the sand from an injury she could not ascertain.

Hugging Hazaq close, Tapat began to weep.

Chapter 11

Andronicus could see his men's concern as they moved back to make room for him to kneel next to Crassus. Crassus was the youngest among them and thus had been adopted by them all as a little brother.

Andronicus glanced quickly at Tapat, the fear that had sliced through him when he saw her attacked making his heart still thrum like a galley war drum. "Are you hurt?"

She shook her head, her bottom lip quivering in an ashen face. Her whole body was shaking, but other than that, she seemed unharmed.

He felt for a pulse in Crassus's neck and found it beating strongly against his fingers. He released a sigh. A pool of blood was forming on the sand beneath his hip, indicating the extent of the injury.

"He's alive," he told them and heard a collective sigh of relief.

"Praise be to Elohim," Tapat cried softly.

Andronicus noticed the catch in Tapat's fervent response. He quickly glanced up and saw the tears shimmering in her eyes. He wondered just how close she and Crassus had become in the past few days. He recognized the feeling clawing its way through his insides and was dismayed by the depth of his jealousy. He turned his attention back to the matter at hand.

"Did anyone see how many got away?" Andronicus asked while carefully turning Crassus over to undo the fastenings for his chest piece. Although the *lorica segmentata* had deflected the slashing sword of his adversary, the weapon had slid down the iron chest piece and sliced through the lower leather section, piercing Crassus's side. The wound was bleeding profusely, although it was fairly superficial, having missed any vital organs. He was more concerned with the gash on the young man's head from hitting a rock when he landed. That was more than likely the reason Crassus was still unconscious, and head gashes tended to bleed heavier than any other kind of wound.

"Four, Tribune," Arius answered and Andronicus heard the displeasure in his voice at having been held back from pursuing them.

Four assailants had survived out of fifteen. He once again felt fervent pride in his men. He doubted the Jews would be back anytime soon, because although they had escaped, they had not done so unscathed. Before moving to Crassus's side, he had noticed a trail of blood leading away from their camp.

He also saw that each of his men was nursing minor injuries, but their concern was more for Crassus.

After removing Crassus's armor, he lifted the side of his blood-red tunic, the symbol of his profession, and revealed the gaping wound in his side. Salvius handed him a cloth retrieved from their supplies. Andronicus tore it in two and used one piece to try to stem the flow of blood coursing from the open wound and the other to mop the blood from his forehead.

Crassus began to stir, and Andronicus almost wished it otherwise. It would be much better for the boy to remain unconscious for what he was going to have to do.

He looked up at Salvius and saw understanding in the other man's eyes.

"Shall I stoke the fire?"

Andronicus nodded, his look grave. "And get me a *pugio.*" The short dagger would be much easier to use as a cautery than the longer gladius.

"What are you going to do?"

Tapat's soft question invaded his worried reflections. With everything happening, he hadn't noticed that the babe had stopped screaming. He quickly sought out the reason and noticed the child had cried himself into exhausted sleep, little hiccuping breaths denoting the trauma he had just been through.

"I have to cauterize the wound," he told her. "Although it's not deep, it will stay open and continue to bleed if it isn't stopped."

He thought she might object, but she nodded in understanding. "Shall I get you some salt?"

"I have it," Salvius said, handing Andronicus the dagger and dropping the bag of salt at his side.

Crassus's eyelids flickered and then opened lethargically. "Tapat?" he questioned in an anxious whisper.

"She is well," Andronicus told him, jealousy once again twining through him like an insidious serpent. "You saved her life."

If he lived to be a hundred years old, he would forever be in this young man's debt for doing so. The thought of Tapat's death chilled him to his very bones.

Tapat got up and came to kneel beside Crassus. Snugly

holding the child with one arm, she reached out and pushed damp tendrils of hair from Crassus's forehead.

"I owe you my life," she told him, but he shook his head.

"No," he rasped. "I owe you much more than that."

Andronicus frowned at the look of understanding that passed between them. What lunacy was this? What could he possibly owe Tapat that was more important than life?

Tapat glanced at Andronicus. "Do you need some help?"

His frown deepened. "No. I need you to move away so I can get this done. Take the child elsewhere."

Her eyes widened and her lips parted in surprise at his surly command. She pressed them together into an uncompromising line. Nodding, she moved away but still remained close.

Crassus, also, was staring at him in astonishment, but he knew better than to comment. Andronicus ignored his inquiring look and placed the *pugio* in the fire.

"You know what I have to do?"

It was more a statement than a question. Crassus swallowed hard and nodded.

Didius stepped forward. "Do you need us to hold him?"

Andronicus lifted a brow at Crassus. It was up to the young man how these seasoned soldiers would perceive him in the future—strong or weak, boy or man. He would not make that decision for him.

Crassus's mouth grew rigid. "I don't need anyone to hold me."

Salvius looked skeptically at Andronicus for confirmation.

"You heard the man," Andronicus told him, putting just the slightest emphasis on the word *man*.

Celsus brought a small stick and handed it to Crassus. Crassus thanked him with a look and placed it between his teeth. His nostrils flared outward as he nodded for Andronicus to do what he must.

Andronicus cleansed the wound first with water from his goatskin. His look held understanding when he saw Crassus tense against the burning pain.

"Ready?"

Crassus nodded, staring upward at the now dark and star-filled sky. Sweat beaded on his brow.

Andronicus pulled the dagger from the fire and, gritting his teeth, slowly pulled it across the wound, searing the edges of the cut together. He winced in sympathy at Crassus's muffled scream. Although Crassus's body jerked slightly, he forced himself to remain still by digging his hands into the desert sand.

Andronicus was impressed with the young man's fortitude. He had known of stronger men than Crassus who cried like a baby when faced with a glowing hot instrument.

He took a handful of salt and carefully packed it around the wound, noting that the burning brought tears to the young man's eyes. More than likely the pain from the salt was worse than the actual cauterization, but it was necessary to stave off infection. He then wrapped a bandage around Crassus's waist, sealing the salt against the burn.

"Well, Didius," Salvius commented, mouth twitching with humor, "I guess it's up to you to milk the goat."

Didius opened his mouth to object, caught Andronicus's look and subsided.

"Seniority," Andronicus reminded him, biting back a grin.

Didius glared at his chuckling companions but went to get the bowl for milking the goat.

Andronicus knew that their merriment was only a ruse to cover the depth of their concern over Crassus's condition. Although such things came with the territory of being a soldier, it wasn't any easier to accept when it was a friend in question. The relief and consequent humor came from knowing that the injury could have been much worse.

He caught Tapat's look. He saw her tears of sympathy, but he also spied a suggestion of joy peeking out from beneath the pain. Something had transpired between her and Crassus that he didn't understand, but he fully intended to find out what it was.

Tapat empathized with Crassus's pain but was elated at what he had hinted to her. The young man had sought out every opportunity to speak with her about the Christian religion, at first to better understand the woman he loved, but then, as they talked more and more, she could see the dawning comprehension in his eyes. He was hungering for a peace that only Christ could give.

The *Pax Romana,* Roman Peace, had brought nothing but savage oppression. True peace was a matter of the heart. Those enslaved to Rome might obey and serve, but an underlying fomenting of rebellion was always just beneath the surface.

Christ-centered peace was a total surrender of the will and came with knowing that you were right with the God who had created you, the God who created a world of order and harmony. Even when surrounded by war, famine, pestilence or other such calamities, there was the serenity of knowing that you could never be taken from the hand of Elohim.

She glanced at Andronicus and her heart responded as it always did when he was near. She knew without a doubt that she would die for him, but she could not live for him. As much as she loved him, she would never allow anything to come between her and the peace she had found in Jesus. How was it that after a few short days Crassus could see what years had not made clear to Andronicus?

Didius brought her a bowl of goat's milk and she thanked him, but she set it aside with a still shaking hand. After such a long time of screaming, Hazaq was sleeping the sleep of the exhausted and she was reluctant to wake him. She would save the milk for when he awoke.

Andronicus made Crassus comfortable near the fire. Despite the oppressive heat, with Crassus being injured, he would surely feel chilled.

The others took the time to move the bodies of those slain to outside of the camp. Tapat had no idea what they were going to do with them. Frankly, she didn't even want to think of it right now. Those sightless eyes were going to haunt her dreams for years to come.

Her people, but not her people. They shared the same race, but not the same beliefs. Still, even though they rejected His Son, she knew they were beloved by Elohim, as were these heathen Romans.

Andronicus gave assignments for the night watch. She noticed that Arius had yet to let down his guard. He stood tensely, searching the area just beyond the perimeter of the firelight. It didn't surprise her that he would wish to continue his watch. Like everyone else, except Hazaq, their nerves were too taut for immediate sleep.

Salvius and Didius set up the tent, and Andronicus came and held out his hand to help her to her feet.

When she placed her hand in his, she felt again that connection that so confused her. He was the only man who had ever made her feel warm and safe yet, paradoxically, unsettled and apprehensive.

He pulled her to her feet but didn't release her right away. She could see all kinds of questions forming in his eyes, questions she was afraid to answer; some she had no answer for.

"Are you sure you're all right?" he asked, glancing over her again. "You're still shaking."

She tugged her hand loose and pulled her gaze away. "I am well."

She could see he continued to search her with narrowed eyes. "I am sorry that you had to witness that."

When she didn't answer, he reached down and picked up the bowl of milk. She walked toward the tent and he followed. She settled on the blanket that had been positioned inside and Andronicus placed the bowl to the side. He then seated himself outside the front entrance.

She could see that he wanted to talk, but her emotions were too raw for her to think clearly. In this state, she would be no match for him if he decided to delve for information.

"I think I will try to get some sleep while Hazaq is doing so," she told him. His tilted smile told her that she hadn't fooled him.

"That's a good idea," he agreed. "I will be here if you need anything."

The silence thrummed between them like an overtightened lyre.

Tapat curled onto the blanket and tried to sleep. An unending stream of images of the day's events kept flashing through her thoughts. She tried to block out the horrific pictures—men in battle, men falling bloody to the ground, the angry Jew who had tried to kill her—but they refused to be stopped.

She finally turned to the only avenue that always brought her peace; she prayed. She prayed for Crassus especially, but also for the rest of them, and that the rest of their journey would be without further hazards.

Elohim had spared Hazaq and she was thankful. She only prayed that He would do the same for the young Roman. She still had so much more to tell him.

Eventually her brain took control and sent her into a deep, cathartic sleep.

Andronicus could hear the change in Tapat's breathing and knew that she was finally asleep.

He hadn't missed the fact that she hadn't wanted to talk to him. She could talk to Crassus for hours on end, but she closed up like a clam whenever he was around. What did they find to talk about that was so interesting? He really wanted to know. He wanted Tapat to open up to him in the same way, and he wanted to see her eyes sparkle with the same shared excitement.

He sat watching her slumber for a long time. Unlike Tapat, his tense nerves fought sleep.

One by one his men finally dozed off, their twitching eyes signaling that their sleep was light. The day's events had put them on guard and it would be some time before they would sleep deeply again.

As for himself, he had no concern that anything more would happen this evening. With Arius on guard, nothing would be able to sneak up on them again tonight. The man could scent an adversary half a league away.

The air grew chillier as the night progressed, a sure sign that they were getting closer to the Jordan River. He leaned into the tent and pulled a blanket over Tapat and the babe.

He brushed the hair away from her face and allowed his fingers to gently glide across her cheek. The action caused her lips to part softly and he jerked his hand away as though burned. His heart, which had finally settled from its erratic beat, once again took up its drumming rhythm.

Shaking his head to clear it of the fog that seemed to be encroaching into his mind, he quickly got up and went to check on Crassus. If the young man could make it through the night without a fever, there was every chance that he wouldn't get one.

He found Crassus awake, his jaw clenched as he tried to hold back any sound that would give away the pain he was in. Andronicus knelt beside him.

"How bad is it?" he asked, wishing that he had thought to bring along some mandragora root. He hadn't given the journey enough thought, believing they would make the trip uneventfully to Pella in just a few days.

"I've had worse."

Not to Andronicus's recollection, but he wouldn't argue with him, knowing he was trying to make light of a trying situation.

Andronicus felt his forehead, relieved that there was still no sign of fever.

"Try to sleep," he admonished softly, hoping that exhaustion would allow Crassus a brief respite from the pain.

Crassus nodded, closing his eyes, more to block out the throbbing, Andronicus was sure, than in belief sleep would come.

He went back to sit outside Tapat's tent. The thought that he had nearly lost her today left him feeling unsettled. He found himself wanting to constantly reach out and touch her just to assure himself that she was, indeed, alive and well.

Hazaq began to stir. Afraid that he would awaken Tapat, and knowing that she needed the sleep, he ducked inside the tent and gently lifted the babe from her side. Tapat frowned in her sleep, moving slightly, and then quieted again.

Slowly releasing a breath, Andronicus hugged the babe close to his side, bent to retrieve the bowl of goat's milk and then took himself outside the tent again.

He sat cross-legged outside the entrance, setting the bowl with the stylus next to him.

Hazaq began squirming more intently, his little face scrunching up into a frown. A sound like the mewling of a cat preceded the opening of his dark, almond eyes.

He blinked up at Andronicus, the frown replaced by a toothless smile. It was at that moment that Andronicus hopelessly lost his heart.

"Hello, little man," he crooned. "Are you hungry?"

He took the stylus and, having seen the way Tapat and Crassus fed the child, managed to give a fairly good attempt. Each day, each hour in fact, saw the child growing stronger and he knew that it had much more to do with Tapat's love and care than anything else.

A long-forgotten memory pushed past the barriers he had erected in his mind. Andronicus was just a boy, still living at home. His mother had a babe, holding it out to his father. His father had folded his arms across his chest, refusing to hold him or give him a name, thereby indicating that the child was not accepted as his son.

His mother had wept softly, but her tears had left his father unmoved. He had ordered the babe taken outside the city and left on the rocks to die. And all because the babe was missing a hand.

It was the Roman way.

Staring down into the face of Hazaq, Andronicus felt those same feelings rush upon him that had swamped him all those years ago—anger and resentment. Had he not been born whole and strong, he would have been rejected, as well.

Perhaps that was why he fought so hard to be the best that he could be in everything he did. Rome would have no compunction about throwing away anything, or anyone, who didn't live up to her standards.

He looked again at Tapat sleeping so peacefully and knew without a doubt that she would never throw away a child no matter what might be wrong with it. Just as she had refused to throw away her mother.

A love so fierce it defied description flowed through him in wave upon wave. He wanted to take her in his arms and hold her forever, protect her from everything.

Chapter 12

Tapat followed along behind the litter carrying Crassus, flinching with him at every bump and rock that jarred the conveyance. His white face and clenched teeth gave mute evidence of the great pain he was in.

She had hoped to find some of the plant that Leah's father, who was a healer, had used to make a balm of oil that he mixed with wine as a sedative. She was uncertain of its actual name, but her people had always called it the balm of Gilead.

Levi taught her how to make the tinctures as well, and she had made use of the knowledge to supply the sedative to those suffering in the Valley of Lepers.

With the arid land drying up earlier than usual because of the intense heat of the *sharav,* the resinous plant was hard to find.

She hoped that the closer they got to the Jordan River, the more abundant the plant might be so she could prepare a sedative to give Crassus some relief from the pain.

She would also prepare a balm to replace the salt on his raw burn.

One thing she looked forward to was being able to immerse herself in the river's cool waters and cleanse herself for the first time in days.

Hazaq had run out of clean swaddling cloths. If she couldn't clean his wraps soon, he would begin to chafe and develop sores.

Andronicus glanced back at Crassus and then at her. Something in his intense expression made her heart stutter, but he turned back without saying a word.

The others constantly searched the area for hidden enemies. The closer they got to the Jordan River, the less likely they would be to encounter nomad Jews. Also, as they neared the plains near the river, the intense heat from the *sharav* lessened.

They finally stopped about midday so that Tapat could feed Hazaq.

Didius made certain that Crassus was situated in the shade of an acacia tree, and Tapat joined him there hoping to help somewhat take his mind off of his pain.

He was staring morosely at the surrounding desert, his mind obviously on something else entirely. She thought she probably knew exactly where that mind was. When he spoke, she was sure of it.

"If I had died, I wonder if Lydia would even have cared."

If Lydia didn't see what a wonderful man Crassus was, she didn't deserve him, but Tapat refrained from saying so. Strange how she had been able to overcome her aversion to the Romans in such a short time. Even the surly and remote Arius had managed to worm his way inside her good graces. Perhaps it had started years ago when she had become enamored of a certain Roman soldier herself.

"I have never met your Lydia," she told him, "but if she is as wonderful as you say, I am sure her feelings would truly be wounded if anything were to happen to you. How could she not? You are a wonderful young man."

Crassus's look went over her shoulder and she turned slowly to find Andronicus standing behind them. The look of fire in his eyes made her tense. What had she done to provoke such a look?

"Feed the babe quickly. We need to be on our way as soon as possible. I want to be across the Jordan Valley before night falls."

He turned on his heels and strode away. Crassus and Tapat exchanged astonished looks. Shrugging her shoulders, Tapat made haste to do as Andronicus suggested. If Crassus didn't understand his commander after years of being in his service, there was no way that she could.

When it was time to leave, Andronicus came to help her onto her horse. She handed Hazaq to Didius, who was standing nearby, and turned to Andronicus. Grasping her by her waist, he lifted her onto the horse. When their eyes met, his dark, possessive gaze made her breath catch in her throat. Her mind told her to look away, but her eyes refused to comply.

Didius watched their silent exchange with lifted brows. Coughing slightly, he interrupted their soundless communication by handing Hazaq into Tapat's waiting arms.

The sun had just begun its downward descent when they finally reached the plains of Jordan. The sand lay out before them, appearing white in the bright sunlight. The area was practically lifeless except for the desert-loving brush scattered throughout. The spring rains were long past and the hot summer was already drying what was left of the blooming plants.

In the distance, the lush fertile banks of the Jordan could be seen and, beyond that, the green and rich mountainous region of the Decapolis.

It took several more hours before they finally reached

the thick, verdant bushes and trees lining the banks of the Jordan River. Tapat gave a long sigh of relief as they moved beneath the canopy of green; the respite from the desert heat was instantaneous.

Andronicus motioned for them to stop. Tapat waited for Didius to come and get Hazaq and then quickly dismounted before Andronicus could help her. One minute Andronicus looked at her as if he wanted to throttle her, the next as if he wanted to…what? What was that disturbing look she had seen in his eyes that made her insides coil and twist like a writhing serpent?

She wasn't certain what she had done to aggravate him earlier, and she didn't intend to wait around and find out. She was in no mood to spar with him right now.

She took Hazaq and headed for the river. The rushing sound of the water was soothing and she longed to plunge into it, but she needed to attend to a few things before she could do so.

Although she was tempted to ignore him, Andronicus's command to wait stopped her in her tracks. She turned to him in question, annoyed with herself when her heart thrummed at an accelerated pace. No matter how much she might wish it otherwise, she couldn't deny the hold he had over her emotions.

He reached her side and looked past her to the tree-shrouded banks of the river.

"The climb down the bank is rather steep. Allow me to carry Hazaq."

She handed the babe over without comment. He held Hazaq with one arm and guided Tapat with his other hand. As she slipped and slid, he seemed as sure-footed as a mountain goat. She envied him the fact that he always seemed so confident of himself.

Tapat found a flat place to lay Hazaq down and hurriedly unwrapped his soiled swaddling cloths, setting them aside to be added to the others. Free of the hot blanket, he kicked his thin legs gleefully and gurgled with happy contentment. Tapat smiled at his play. He was such a sweet little babe.

She ran her hands gently over his arms and legs, noting with sadness that they were not putting on any weight. Although the goat's milk had helped him to survive, he wasn't getting enough sustenance to nourish his body. She didn't know what else to do. He was much too young to feed solid foods.

Andronicus seated himself cross-legged beside her.

He gently chucked Hazaq under the chin with his finger and the babe squealed, grabbing the offending appendage. Tapat saw the softening of Andronicus's countenance and her heart melted. One moment he could be fierce and brutal and the next soft and gentle.

It was hard to relate this man to the same one who had ruthlessly brandished his sword last night, annihilating his opponents swiftly and effectively. She was beginning to see more and more the facets of his character, each one more compelling than the last. But this switching back and forth between the two was leaving her dizzy.

"He is a beautiful child," he told her softly, allowing Hazaq to chew on his finger.

He glanced up and caught her look before she had time to school her features. His eyes darkened as he searched hers for something, but she couldn't fathom what he was looking for.

The silence between them lengthened, humming with unasked questions.

They were interrupted by the men bringing the horses down to the river to drink. Celsus knelt to fill the water flasks.

"Are we going to make camp here tonight?" he asked, standing and hoisting the filled bags over his shoulders.

Andronicus shook his head. "No. We'll camp on the

other side. I only stopped here to give the horses a rest after the hot trip across the valley."

Arius studied the flowing river. "It doesn't look very deep here. It will be a good place to cross." He looked at Andronicus. "Still, Crassus will have to ride."

It was true. The litter couldn't be dragged through the water. Though somewhat shallow at this point, the river was still too deep for the conveyance. Tapat opened her mouth to object but was interrupted by Crassus's voice preceding him.

"I will be fine."

Crassus slowly made his way down to them, one arm curled around his injured middle, the other using the various trees for support. With every step, his face whitened further.

Tapat jumped to her feet. "Are you demented? You should be lying down!"

He smiled wryly. "There is only one babe on this journey, and it is not I."

Tapat glared at Andronicus. "Tell him!"

She couldn't understand the look that crossed Andronicus's face, nor the one he exchanged with Crassus. "I think perhaps Crassus knows best what he can and can't handle."

She looked at each man in turn for support but could find no one willing to agree with her. What was it with men? Were they so afraid of being seen as weak that they would risk permanent injury to themselves to prove otherwise? Glowering in frustration at each of them, she picked Hazaq up and flounced farther downstream. Let them have each other's company; she was fed up with the lot of them.

Holding Hazaq under his arms, she dipped his legs into the water. At the unexpected coolness, his eyes widened in surprise. He pulled his legs up, squealing and then, laughing, started kicking his feet in the water. Tapat laughed with him when his antics drenched them both.

Andronicus followed her. He was undaunted by the look she gave him. His lips twitched with amusement, rekindling the ashes of her anger. She saw nothing humorous in his taking Crassus's side over hers.

"We will be ready to leave in a few minutes. Do what you need to, and come back."

"What about washing Hazaq's clothes?"

"We will make camp on the other side of the river in Decapolis territory. You can take care of it then."

He turned and headed back to where the soldiers waited. She took the opportunity to make use of the surrounding trees to answer nature's call before wrapping Hazaq in her shawl and returning to the others.

Andronicus took the reins to Tapat's horse, while Didius took the reins of Crassus's. Although it was mere feet to the other side, with each jolting move, Crassus's face grew paler and Tapat feared he would fall from his mount into the water. Celsus must have had the same idea because he spurred his horse next to Crassus, maintaining his distance but ready to steady him if needed.

Tapat clung tightly to her own horse with her legs as they moved down into the river. She grasped Hazaq so tightly, the child eventually let her know with a sudden shriek that he didn't appreciate the confining hold. She only slightly loosened her hold on him while maintaining her own grip on her horse.

The river was calm at this location, rising only as far as the horse's belly. It took only a few moments to cross to the other side, and Tapat released a relieved breath when they finally stopped again.

Andronicus led them out of the dense foliage lining the banks and into a level section where they could make camp. He relaxed, knowing there was little possibility of attack on this side of the Jordan. They were in Decapolis territory, and the Decapolis cities made certain that the area was free of Jewish or Arab invaders.

The Decapolis cities had maintained their Greek identities despite having been taken over by Maccabean rule and then later by the Romans under Pompey. They clung fiercely to Greek ways, and Rome allowed them their independence with only minor interference. They were even allowed their own system of defense and, being small cities, they combined their forces to protect their borders.

Which was probably why the Christians had decided to settle here. From what he had learned from his spies in Jerusalem, after the purge of Christians by the Jews, most Christians in the area were now Gentiles. They would have no problem fitting in with the Greek cities despite the many idols littering the streets and buildings.

A startled exclamation from Tapat brought his attention to her. She was hurrying to a small cluster of bushes.

"What's wrong?" he asked, making his way to her side. She handed him Hazaq.

"Nothing is wrong. I have found what I need to make a sedative for Crassus."

Andronicus frowned. Tapat's strong concern for the younger soldier worried him. They seemed to grow closer with each passing mile, whereas he and she seemed to be growing farther apart. Why had Tapat put such distance between them while allowing herself a closer bond with Crassus?

"May I use your dagger?"

He handed it to her without thought, reminding himself just how much he trusted her. He only wished that she would feel the same way about him.

She knelt, glancing at him over her shoulder while hacking away at the plant. "Will you feed Hazaq while I prepare the medicine?"

He nodded, smiling down at the cooing babe. "Are you hungry, little man?"

He waited until Tapat was satisfied that she had enough of the plant and then walked with her to where the others had already set up camp. Celsus stood first guard while the others found places to sleep.

Andronicus settled himself near the tent and prepared to feed Hazaq while watching Tapat.

She peeled the bark from the plant she had collected, releasing the resin underneath. Then, filling a clay bowl with water, she added the bark, setting the whole thing in the fire to boil.

He recognized the other plant she lifted from beside her. Aloe was a common medicinal plant.

Glancing over at Crassus, he saw that he slept fitfully near the fire, unaware of Tapat's absorbed attention on preparing something to relieve his pain. She squeezed some of the aloe's tissue onto a rag and added several drops of the resin from the other plant.

Hazaq's sucking grew less urgent as he became satisfied. Each time the little fellow closed his eyes, he would jerk awake and begin sucking again until, finally, his eyes stayed closed, his breathing deepened and his little body became a dead weight, telling Andronicus that he was asleep at last.

He wasn't certain what they were going to do with the little babe. Although the goat's milk was keeping him alive, he was on a razor-thin edge. His little body was not growing as it should because he couldn't get enough sustenance by just sucking dropperfuls at a time. Perhaps when they got to Pella they could figure out a better way to nourish him. Mayhap they would even find a wet nurse.

Andronicus placed Hazaq on the blanket in the tent, taking a moment to rub a calloused finger across his downy little cheek. Who would this innocent little child grow up to be? So many scenarios played through his mind, none of them to his liking. There was no denying that the babe had wormed his way into Andronicus's heart. It was going to be a wrench to leave him.

After exiting the tent, Andronicus went and stood next to Tapat, who was kneeling beside Crassus.

"How is he?"

She shook her head as she used a cloth to wipe the perspiration from Crassus's forehead. "He has the beginning of a fever."

That was certainly not a good sign. Andronicus knelt beside her. "What do you want to do?"

"I need to remove the wrapping around his wound, but I hate to awaken him when I know how exhausted and weak he must be."

Andronicus gently shook the other man's shoulder. "Crassus. Wake up."

Recognizing the commanding voice, Crassus's eyes quickly opened. Andronicus's mouth tilted into a lopsided smile. Even asleep and with a fever, he still recognized his commander's voice. It was drummed into them early in their training, as was the ability to focus in spite of injury or pain.

Despite his earlier reservations about Crassus, he had proved his worth time and time again. With each passing day, he grew fonder of the boy. Andronicus had no doubt in his mind that Crassus would willingly die for those he was loyal to. Perhaps it was not so hard to understand Tapat's concern after all; Crassus had bestowed on her the same fierceness of devotion that he had for his legion. He felt a sharp pang at the thought and recognized it for the jealousy that it was.

"Tribune?" Crassus questioned in a raspy voice. He tried to rise, but Tapat gently pushed him back.

"It's all right, Crassus," she soothed. "We merely need to change your bandage."

He settled back with a sigh, his eyes rolling back into his head.

Andronicus lifted Crassus's tunic, exposing his loin cloth. Tapat colored hotly, turning her face away.

"Do you want me to do it?" Andronicus asked her.

She shook her head, swallowing down her discomfort. "No, I need you to bring me some water to wash away the salt."

He hesitated. "Are you certain?"

She nodded, focusing her attention on removing the bandage.

Andronicus retrieved the flask of water and handed it to her. As gently as possible, she poured it over the wound as she wiped away the crystals of salt at the same time. Crassus sucked in his breath, his hands clutching the blanket he lay upon.

Tapat lightly and carefully smoothed the balm mixture over the wound. It took only moments before Crassus's body relaxed, his teeth slowly unclenching.

"Better?" Tapat asked him, once again wiping the perspiration from his face.

He nodded tightly, and Tapat set about rewrapping the wound.

Tapat looked up at Andronicus. "I need a cup of wine."

With a quick jerk of the head in affirmation, he quickly retrieved the flask that contained the fermented drink. Tapat then added it to the resinous liquid in the bowl she had placed in the fire. When the mixture had cooled enough, she helped Crassus to sit up enough to drink the gall, then helped him to settle back against the blanket.

"In a few moments, you should feel an ease of the pain and be able to sleep."

He gave her a grateful smile. "Thank you."

She waited until she was certain Crassus was asleep before she left from his side. Andronicus lifted a brow in question.

"What now?"

"Now," Tapat said wearily, gathering up the dirty laundry, "I need to wash Hazaq's swaddling cloths."

Andronicus took them from her and she looked at him in surprise.

"Why don't you wash your own clothes and take a bath in the river?" He had seen the yearning in her eyes ever since they had reached the Jordan. "I will wash Hazaq's clothing."

Her brow lifted dubiously and he grinned. "I'm not helpless, you know. I do know how to wash linen strips."

She still looked uncertain. "If you are sure."

"I am. You may move over into the darkness, but stay close enough that I can hear you if you call."

She glanced at the soiled cloths and then back at the river longingly. Finally giving in to the desire, she smiled in capitulation. She grabbed a blanket from the tent to wrap herself in while her clothing dried and hurried past him into the darker area of the river just beyond the campfire.

Andronicus moved down to the water's edge and began dipping the cloths up and down in the water. He found a rock to pound them on and continued pounding and wringing while surreptitiously watching Tapat's shadowy figure in the darkness beyond.

He heard her singing, her soft, musical voice more soothing than the moving water. The words were about her Christ, her Savior who had died on a Roman cross. For some reason, the words reached deep into the inner recesses of his mind and conjured up pictures that he would like to forget.

In front of Jerusalem right this very minute many more

crosses lined the roads, crosses with people screaming in pain.

Such things had been a part of his life for many years, so why was it bothering him so much now? The curious words of the song penetrated his musing.

Faith is being sure of what we hope for and certain of what we do not see.

What kind of mixed up nonsense was that? The only thing he was certain of was that this woman had tied him up in knots and he didn't know how to extricate himself—or even if he wanted to.

He snorted in derision, reminding himself again that he was in the middle of a war. He didn't have time for romance.

Chapter 13

They traveled northward following the river's course. Two wearying days later they reached the outer region of the city of Pella.

Tapat was relieved to see that Crassus no longer flinched in pain with every plodding step. The balm had worked, and with the aloe, his wound was healing. The fever she had been worrying over ceased to exist, and she attributed that to prayer more than anything.

As they passed through a wooded area beside the Jordan and close to the city, they heard voices off to their left. The soldiers, including Crassus, tensed and drew their swords swiftly from their scabbards. His fierce countenance gave no indication of pain.

Tapat marveled at the endurance of Roman soldiers. Somehow, they willed themselves to ignore even excruciating pain when faced with the possibility of conflict. It was no wonder that Rome had conquered most of the known world when it commanded men like that.

"Stay here," Andronicus commanded Tapat and, together with his troops, he slowly headed in the direction of the voices.

Tapat sat frozen to the spot, tightening her hold on Hazaq. Terrible images she had been trying her best to forget resurfaced in her mind. "Please, Lord. Not again," she whispered.

Voices drifted to her on the calm morning air, and her eyes widened in surprise. People were singing a hymn. Recognizing the words, Tapat was suddenly filled with overwhelming joy. Praise the Lord, she had found the very ones she had been seeking.

Ignoring Andronicus's command, she carefully slid from the horse so as not to drop Hazaq and followed in Andronicus's direction.

When she reached a clearing in the trees, she could see Andronicus and the men sitting quietly on their horses watching a group of people clustered on the banks of the river. There were both men and women, elderly and young. The tunics they wore spoke of both poverty and wealth.

Two men were standing in the river, one gray and elderly, the other just past youth. The elderly man had his hand on the back of the other. Realizing what was happening, Tapat hurried forward.

Andronicus noticed her and told her to stop, but she ignored him and continued on.

At his commanding voice, the area went quiet. The people turned to stare, their eyes widening in alarm when they recognized the Roman uniforms.

Tapat saw her friend Mary among the crowd.

"Mary!" she called, waving frantically. Before she could move farther, Andronicus stood and blocked her way. She glanced up at him in surprise. So intent had she been on reaching her friend, she hadn't even noticed that he'd left his horse.

"What do you think you are doing?" he demanded angrily.

"It's all right," she told him, looking past him to the others. "They are my friends."

Andronicus glanced over his shoulder, lifting a brow in question. She couldn't blame him. They didn't look particularly welcoming. Even Mary was hesitant to greet her in the light of her present company.

She tried to move around Andronicus, but his stance was unyielding. Using the opportunity afforded her, she handed him Hazaq.

"Here. Hold him."

Taken by surprise, he had to cuddle the babe close to keep from dropping him. While his attention was diverted, Tapat quickly dodged around him and hurried to the now murmuring crowd.

"Mary," she called again, but Mary was too frightened to acknowledge her.

Tapat's steps slowed. She searched the faces for others she might recognize. Some she had seen before in Jerusalem, but that had been three years ago.

"It's all right," she informed them. "These men mean you no harm. They are my friends."

"You keep strange friends," a voice from the crowd whispered, and Tapat felt the hackles on her neck rise in anger. She glared at the crowd, but instead of lashing out, she remembered her own feelings about these men not so very long ago.

"I have come from Jerusalem," she told them in frustration. "I am no spy. Mary knows who I am."

Finally getting up her courage, Mary nodded to an older man in the group Tapat supposed was one of the congregational leaders. His white hair and kind brown eyes reminded her of the Apostle John, who she had once met.

He stepped forward, stopping when he glanced over her shoulder.

Turning slightly, Tapat found Andronicus standing behind her and holding Hazaq close. The look he gave her seared her more thoroughly than the *sharav* heat that had scorched them for much of the way here. Ignoring his anger, she told the elderly man, "These are my friends. They traveled here with me to assure my safety. My name is Tapat."

He studied her silently for several seconds, looking deep into her eyes for the honesty of her statement. She had the feeling that nothing could be hidden from his discerning eyes. When he smiled, it reduced his apparent old age by years.

"Welcome, then, little sister." He looked from Andronicus to the others waiting just behind. "You are all welcome to join us in our celebration. Democides has just this morning decided to put on the Lord in baptism, and then we will adjourn to my house and celebrate the Lord's Day of the Lord together. My name is Jason, by the way."

Tapat's eyes widened. So much had happened in the past several days she had lost track of the days. It had been a long time since she had been able to worship with other believers. Joy rippled through her, making her want to join them in lifting her voice in praise.

"I wish to be baptized."

Recognizing the voice, Tapat turned to find Crassus standing just behind Andronicus. Andronicus whirled around so quickly it startled Hazaq, and he began to whimper. Tapat and Andronicus both stared at Crassus in astonishment.

With a squeal, Tapat threw herself into the boy's arms and hugged him exuberantly. He flinched, sucking in a sharp breath at the pain she caused him but stoically enduring her congratulations.

Jason stared at them all with uncertainty. "You believe

that Jesus is the Christ, the Son of the living God?" he asked Crassus skeptically.

"I believe." There was no denying the conviction in his voice.

"Crassus." Andronicus's voice held a warning. Crassus looked at his commander, his face filled with determination. They could hear the murmuring of the other soldiers mixed with the astonished murmurings of the crowd.

Jason glanced from Crassus to Andronicus and back again. It was clear that he was uncertain how to proceed.

Tapat laid her hand on the old man's arm. "I have been studying with Crassus. If he says he believes, then it is so." They locked eyes, and once again Tapat felt as though the old man could see into her very soul.

Jason looked at Andronicus. "Then I have no objection."

Andronicus handed the now fussing Hazaq to Tapat. She tried to reassure him with her eyes that everything would be all right, but he refused to look at her.

"Are you certain that you want to go down this path?" he asked Crassus.

Crassus took a deep breath. "I am certain."

"Then so be it."

He turned and walked back to the others, his stiff back speaking clearly of his feelings on the matter. Climbing onto his horse, he sat waiting for Tapat and Crassus to return to their own mounts, ignoring the heated remonstrances from his men.

The crowd parted as Crassus moved between them, heading for the river. When he reached the shore, he took off his gladius and armor, leaving only his blood-red tunic and hobnailed boots. Even without his armor, and despite his youth, he was impressive.

He glanced at Tapat, and she came and briefly clutched his hand. A look of understanding passed between them. From this time forth, he would be her brother in the Lord.

He walked into the water with the other men. They threw him uneasy glances but returned to their business.

"On your confession of faith in our Lord Jesus, Democides, I now baptize you in the name of the Father, the Son and the Holy Spirit for the forgiveness of your sins."

With that, the old man lay Democides back, plunging him beneath the Jordan's moving waters. When he lifted him up again, Democides smiled through the water running down his face. The two hugged and Democides moved up to the shore to be embraced by the joyous crowd.

The old man glanced hesitantly at Crassus but motioned him forward.

"I didn't catch your name," he said in embarrassment.

"Crassus."

Nodding, the old man then placed a hand on Crassus's back. "On your confession of faith in our Lord Jesus, Crassus, I now baptize you in the name of the Father, the Son and the Holy Spirit for the forgiveness of your sins."

Andronicus watched as Crassus was plunged beneath the river, his feelings a riot of confusion. As the boy's commander, he was hesitant to give his consent to the proceedings. He should have tried to dissuade the boy from taking such a step but, met with such determination, he had no choice but to concede. Reprisal would come later, no doubt. Although his men had tolerated Tapat as the Christian she was, he had no doubt that they would feel much differently about Crassus. It would be hard to trust your back to someone who spoke of loving your enemies.

When Crassus rose from the water, his drenched face was filled with undeniable joy. The first person he searched for was Tapat. She stood nearby holding Hazaq, tears running down her cheeks, her face mirroring Crassus's joy.

Andronicus again felt that serpent of jealousy writhing

its way through him. With Crassus's acceptance of Tapat's God, there was nothing to keep them apart. Unlike him.

His jealousy was mixed with confusion. An aura of peace mixed with the joy that now filled Crassus's face. The same peace he had always seen in Tapat regardless of circumstances. How did plunging beneath water bring a person such happiness? He had seen the same thing in his friend Lucius. If he asked, would Tapat give him the answer as readily as she gave it to Crassus?

Crassus climbed from the river and gathered his gear. The people on the bank were swarming him and the other man, Democides, hugging and smiling. With that one act, Crassus had gone from being a foe to being a friend. Andronicus shook his head at the lunacy of it.

Jason walked over to Andronicus. "If you will follow me to my house, we will help you and your men get situated. And if it is not too much to ask, the church elders would like to meet with you and Tapat for a few minutes."

Andronicus felt himself bristle. Something in the man's tone put his teeth on edge. He was fairly certain that although the words were innocuous enough, it was not a request. But Tapat's future depended on these people, so he pushed down his irritation and nodded.

Crassus held Hazaq while Tapat remounted, then he handed her the bundle and climbed onto his own horse. They all followed the Christians through the column-lined streets of Pella. It was a beautiful city, more Greek than Roman. Statues of the gods in their Greek and Roman forms lined the streets.

They passed through the forum, where most of the businessmen of the city had gathered, and by the civic center, where in the amphitheater a play by Ovid was taking place. Everywhere they went, people stopped and stared.

Jason finally stopped before a large villa. He opened the gate in the outer wall and motioned for everyone to precede him. The affluence of the place was apparent on first entering the gate. Seldom had Andronicus seen such a beautiful home, even in Rome.

Servants came to take the horses.

Andronicus pulled off his helmet and tucked it under his arm. He was longing to take advantage of the public bath, but that would have to wait.

Tapat started to walk by him, but he reached out and grasped her upper arm. "Jason says that the elders would like to speak to us."

She looked at him in surprise. "Now? But it is the Lord's Day of the Lord. It's time to worship."

Jason overheard and came to their side. "Tapat is correct. It *is* time to worship. You are welcome to join us."

Andronicus glared at the man. "I think not. My men and I will find accommodations in the city." He looked at Tapat. "I assume you are staying?"

She nodded, her eyes pleading with him to reconsider. Turning away, he asked, "When did you wish to meet?"

Jason glanced from Andronicus to Tapat. "Can you come back this evening?"

Andronicus nodded. He would take full advantage of the baths and then find a place to settle himself and his men for the night.

"I wish to remain for a time, Tribune," Crassus told him.

Andronicus hesitated before finally relenting. "As you wish."

Andronicus pulled Tapat to the side and out of the hearing of the others. He searched her face carefully. "Will you be all right?"

He saw in her eyes her reluctance for him to leave and he found himself loathe to do so, but he intended to do some scouting around and find out about these Christians before he would be willing to leave Tapat in their hands for long. He cupped her cheek with his palm, stroking his thumb across her lips. The pupils of her eyes darkened in response and he smiled inwardly. She was not as unaffected as she pretended to be.

"I will be fine." Hazaq began to fuss and Tapat pulled away from Andronicus's touch. "I must see to Hazaq."

She had pulled away from him mentally and physically, but he was too experienced in the ways of women to be fooled. She *was* attracted to him.

"I will return this evening."

The look that flashed through her eyes this time was easy to interpret.

"I promise," he reiterated, and she nodded apprehensively.

As he followed his men out the door, he turned one last time and saw Tapat still standing where he had left her.

Chapter 14

The day had been long and tiring despite the enjoyment of being able to worship the Lord with other believers. Worshipping here in Pella was much like doing so in Jerusalem, except without the fear of reprisal.

Taking the Lord's Supper had been the highlight of the service for Tapat. It had been so long since she had been able to commune with Elohim that way. It was always during this time that she became reverently introspective, searching her mind and heart to make certain that she did not partake in an unworthy manner as the Apostle Paul had warned about.

Several people had confessed their sins to one another and had been lovingly embraced by those in attendance.

The singing had been wonderful. So many voices joined together in joyous worship had brought tears to her eyes.

When it came time to pray, Tapat had silently thanked Elohim for bringing her here safely. She listened attentively as the elders prayed for others of the congregation who were ill or in need. When she heard her own name mentioned, she jerked her head up in surprise. Even Crassus had been mentioned, warming her heart at their acceptance of him. She reached over and squeezed his hand, smiling when he returned the pressure.

The fellowship had gone on for hours. It was only as the sun was beginning its descent that Jason had come to her and offered her a room to use until she could decide what she wanted to do. She had accepted gratefully, not certain now what she was going to do with her life. She still had the money that Andronicus had given her, so she would be able to support herself and Hazaq, but it would take time to find a place for them to live. She had long ago decided that he was her responsibility. Elohim had placed him in her path for a reason, and she would not turn her back on such a gift.

Tapat marveled at the beauty of the peristyle a servant led her through. The garden was full of blooming flowers and lush green trees. A flame tree in the corner was losing its last scarlet flowers to the early summer.

The sound of running water was soothing as a fountain in the center spewed water from a beautifully carved statue of a young man carrying a pitcher over his shoulder.

Everything in this villa spoke of extreme wealth, and she suddenly wondered what kind of occupation Jason held or if he was independently wealthy, like her former mistress.

A balcony ran the entire length of the upper-floor rectangle of the peristyle, where doors to many rooms opened onto the garden. Below the balcony the lower floor held just as many doors. The servant stopped just outside one of these doors and pushed open the wooden portal.

"This will be your room, my lady."

Tapat followed her inside. The room boasted a large sleeping couch, a luxury after the many nights of sleeping on the hard ground. It was lavishly supplied with silken sheets and pillows.

A dressing table sported a polished silver mirror, the likes of which she hadn't seen since leaving Leah's service. On the table were several amphorae of scented oils, a comb and a brush.

Several oil braziers were scattered around the room, ready to be lit when darkness settled over the land. Potted plants perched on intricately carved pedestals.

"Is it to your liking?"

Tapat turned to the young servant. What wasn't to like? It was a room lushly appointed, obviously used for guests. "Very much so. Thank you…?"

"Euphemia," she supplied.

"Thank you, Euphemia."

Euphemia nodded. "If you are ready, I will show you and the baby to the baths."

Another luxury she looked forward to. She followed the servant down a long corridor that ended in a large bathroom. Several other women were already in the pool visiting in friendly camaraderie. Embarrassed, Tapat hesitated. She had never gotten used to community baths, although they had been a part of her master's life when she had been a slave in Caesarea. She did not understand how men and women could prance naked before each other when not married or even related. It was just one more thing that set the Jews apart from the Romans—their modesty.

At least no men were here. Jason might be living as a Greek, but he was still a Christian, and the Lord and the Apostles had warned about modesty and lusting.

Euphemia started to help her remove her tunic but Tapat shook her head. "If you would hold Hazaq for me?"

Smiling, Euphemia reached for Hazaq, cuddling him close and cooing at him even though the odor that emanated from him couldn't have been pleasant.

"If you would like, I will bathe him for you," she suggested.

Again Tapat hesitated. It would be difficult to wash her hair and body and hang on to a squirming child at the same time. She finally nodded her head in assent and Euphemia started unwrapping Hazaq's swaddling cloths.

Tapat pulled her tunic over her head, holding it against her front modestly. She eased her way into the tepidarium, the warm water pool instantly soothing her aching muscles. Leaving her tunic on the surrounding tiled floor, she ducked beneath the water to completely wet her hair. When she rose again, a woman was standing where her tunic had been. The garment was gone. She glanced up at the woman in surprise.

Before she could speak, the woman told her, "My name is Nivia. Jason is my husband. I hope you don't mind, but I have had your tunic removed to be cleaned." She laid a yellow tunic on the tiles. "I hope you will accept this tunic in its place."

Embarrassed, Tapat gave her a hesitant smile. "I can pay you."

Nivia shook her head, returning her smile. "That is not necessary. We keep such garments for just such a purpose."

Tapat wasn't certain she understood, but she nodded her head in acceptance. "Thank you."

She quickly searched for Hazaq and saw Euphemia bringing him over, cleaned and wrapped once again in clean swaddling cloths. He was beginning to fuss and Tapat knew that he was hungry. She was going to have to find out what they had done with the goat and her bag with the stylus.

"As soon as you are finished, my husband and the other elders would like a word with you in the bibliotheca. Euphemia will show you the way." Nivia patted the girl's shoulder and Euphemia smiled up at her. "I will leave you now."

Tapat watched her walk away and felt a sudden sense of

loss that was ridiculous under the circumstances. Perhaps it was the fact that Nivia reminded her so much of her own mother; even her coloring was the same.

Shaking herself from her fanciful thoughts, she hurried to finish her bath. She didn't want to keep the elders waiting. Ignoring the looks from the other women, she climbed the steps out of the bath and quickly dried herself off.

Andronicus stood in Jason's bibliotheca and looked around at the numerous scrolls in their cubbyholes. His library was extensive, one of the largest Andronicus had ever seen.

Jason and two other men came into the room, followed by servants bringing in more stools. Andronicus felt much like when he was called to come before the emperor.

Jason motioned to a chair. "Please, have a seat."

Andronicus did so, looking around for Tapat. He lifted an eyebrow at the three men. Understanding the unasked question, Jason told him, "Tapat will be here momentarily."

The words were no more out of his mouth than Tapat walked into the room.

Andronicus's jaw dropped. Somehow in the past week Tapat had gone from being a dewy-eyed innocent to a woman of strong purpose. Her features had taken on a look of maturity that made one think she was a woman to be reckoned with. What had brought about such a change? He was sorry to see the one disappear, but this new woman's eyes glowed with an intent that made him sit up and take notice.

A soft yellow tunic clung to her feminine curves as she gracefully crossed the floor in her bare feet to stand, cuddling Hazaq, before the three men. Her still damp hair cascaded down her back in a soft black curtain, clean and shining once again.

Andronicus swallowed hard and turned away, catching Jason's eye. The other man was watching him intently, searching for something that Andronicus hoped hadn't been visible on his face. Desire had flashed through him unlike anything he had ever experienced before. He donned the mask that had served him so well over the years, his features turning to stone.

Jason indicated that Tapat should sit. Moving to the vacant seat next to Andronicus, she perched lightly on the edge of the stool.

Andronicus reached over and stroked Hazaq's hand, and the child grasped his finger, grinning toothlessly up at him. He grinned in return, but at a slight cough from across the room, he gave his attention back to the three men.

Steepling his fingers in front of him, Jason bid them to tell their story. Andronicus opened his mouth to do so but was preempted when Tapat began speaking. As he listened to her telling the story, he couldn't help but think that it would make a good play for a Greek tragedy. He also realized just how unbelievable it sounded.

When she came to the part about Martha and Hazaq, the three men glanced at each other, their faces a study in astonishment. The look they exchanged left Andronicus slightly unsettled. They were concealing something, their eyes glittering with excitement.

When Tapat finished her story, she sat waiting expectantly for them to say something. When they did, it was not what either of them had expected.

The older man sitting next to Jason, who had introduced himself as Claudius, smiled at Tapat. "Surely you are an answer to our prayers, and we to yours."

Andronicus's eyes narrowed skeptically. Tapat stared at them curiously.

"Let me explain," Jason interrupted, giving the other man a warning look. He turned back to Tapat and hesitated several seconds before he said anything else. He glanced at the other two men. "Perhaps it would be better to show her."

They nodded their heads vigorously in approval. Jason motioned a servant over. "Find Timothy and Bernice and bring them here."

When the servant had gone, Jason looked again at Tapat. "Two weeks ago, our sister, Bernice, and her husband, Timothy, lost their baby. We are uncertain what happened. They just awoke and found one morning that he had gone to be with the Lord."

Tapat's face was a picture of horror. She glanced down at Hazaq, cuddling him even closer. It didn't take much to be able to read her mind. Although Hazaq wasn't her birth child, Tapat would be devastated if something happened to him. What she would do if Hazaq did not survive had concerned Andronicus the entire trip.

Before Jason could speak further, the servant reentered the room followed by a young couple. The man gently led the woman into the room, his solicitous attitude speaking of great love. The woman, however, was entirely different. Andronicus had seen more life in a corpse.

"You sent for us?" the man, Andronicus assumed him to be Timothy, asked, never taking his eyes off the woman.

Hazaq cried and the woman, Bernice, quickly looked up. Her eyes lit on Hazaq's squirming form and tears pooled in them. She looked longingly at Tapat, her lifeless eyes now sparking with interest. "Is he yours?"

Andronicus noticed Tapat's hesitation and realized that to answer affirmatively would be for her to lie, something he couldn't imagine her doing. She looked to him for help.

His scrutiny encompassed the occupants of the room, ending with Hazaq. He knew with sudden conviction what these men were suggesting. Truly it would be an answer to the problem. With Bernice having lost her child such a short time ago and Hazaq struggling to feed through a reed straw, the solution was obvious.

He looked at Tapat and saw when she realized exactly what was happening. Her eyes opened wide and she slowly began to shake her head from side to side. "No," she breathed softly.

Jason half rose, intending to speak. Andronicus silenced him with a quick motion of the hand, and he settled back into his seat. Their gazes collided.

Andronicus stood, glancing down at Tapat. "If you would all leave the room, I would like to speak with Tapat alone."

He knew that he had some gall making such demands in a house that wasn't his own, but right now he didn't care. His only concern was for Tapat and Hazaq.

"I think that's a good idea," Jason agreed, rising from his seat. The others followed suit; Timothy led Bernice out the door last, as she continued to look yearningly at Hazaq.

Andronicus stared at Tapat hovering protectively over Hazaq. He knew what he had to do for both her sake and the child's.

"Tapat?"

She angrily shook her head. "Don't even suggest it!" she practically snarled, pulling Hazaq closer.

He seated himself beside her again and took her hand. She tried to pull it away, but he wouldn't allow it. He could feel her shaking and, without thinking about the consequences, pulled her and Hazaq across his lap, holding them as one would when comforting a child.

She sobbed softly into his shoulder and Hazaq began to fuss, sensing her distress. "I can't. Please don't ask it of me."

"*Carrisima,* we have to think of Hazaq. He can't continue the way he is or he will die. You know that. He's not getting enough to eat."

She sobbed harder, and he thought his heart would break for her.

"Can't you see that this is all a part of your God's plan?

Aren't you the one who has always told me that all things work together for the good of those who love your Lord?"

She stared up at him in astonishment, the sobbing lessening but the tears still running in an unending stream.

"Yes, *bella*," he told her softly, "I have been listening to you."

She searched his eyes for several seconds before her face crumpled once more. She buried her face in his chest again.

"I can't, Andronicus! I just can't!"

He held her tighter, placing his cheek against the top of her head. His own throat clogged with suppressed tears. He had grown to love the little boy, as well. How was it that he hadn't considered what parting with the child and Tapat was truly going to mean? It was suddenly tearing him apart to even think about it. But he had to consider what was best for everyone, and so did she. A boy needed a father, and a single mother would have a hard time supporting herself and a child. And Bernice could give the child what he needed most now: nourishment to grow and thrive.

"Yes, you can, *mea amo*," he whispered harshly.

Tapat dropped her head back, the pleading in her eyes not reaching her lips. He cupped her chin with his hand. "Yes, you can," he repeated much softer. "You had the strength to keep him. Now you need to have the strength to let him go."

Hazaq's crying grew louder. Tapat slid from Andronicus's lap and stood. Her face had gone from strong and sure of purpose to hopeless and haggard with grief. She stared forlornly down at the child before raining kisses across his face and, in an action that took Andronicus by surprise, handed Hazaq to him.

"I can't do it!" she cried and ran from the room, leaving Hazaq with him. He realized just what she was saying by her action. It was up to him to be strong for both of them. He swallowed hard against the lump forming in his throat.

Jason and the others returned to the room, their questioning looks going from Andronicus to Tapat as she fled down the hallway.

Andronicus got up and went to Bernice. Her eyes were focused hungrily on Hazaq, and there was more life in them than when she had first entered the room. He had to believe that this was for the best.

Jason met his look with understanding. The older man nodded slightly, giving him the courage to do what must be done.

He kissed Hazaq, and without saying anything, he handed the child to Bernice, leaving it to Jason to explain further. He quickly followed Tapat's fleeing figure.

Chapter 15

Andronicus found Tapat sitting next to her favorite place—the waterfall that tumbled over the mountain to the Jordan River flowing in the distance. She was staring out over the lush green hills, the mist from the waterfall creating a beautiful rainbow in the chasm below.

He had followed her here the night they had arrived and she had fled from Jason's house after relinquishing possession of Hazaq. He knew at the time that she was blinded by her tears and wouldn't pay attention to where she was going; she just needed to escape.

Following a safe distance behind her, he had imprinted landmarks in his memory while instinctively knowing that she needed the space as she struggled with her fragmented emotions.

The rushing water had at last impeded her progress and she had stopped and fallen to the ground, her sobs tearing him apart inside. Although she had tried to push him away, he had lifted her from the ground and wrapped his arms about her, snugging her head beneath his chin.

He had held her for several long hours, until her copious weeping had been reduced to intermittent sniffles, and then he continued to hold her beyond what was probably advisable. That night, he had been the friend she needed. Now the sound of the rushing water couldn't even begin to compare to the blood roaring through him as he saw her sitting there. Friendship was the farthest thing from his mind.

It was time to return to Jerusalem, but he couldn't bring himself to do so until he was certain that Tapat was well.

At his approach, she turned, looked up at him and gave him a tired smile. Despite the dark circles under her eyes, he marveled at her serene features and realized that he had interrupted her communing with her God. It always unnerved him when he saw her like this. At these times, he felt a great gulf between them and, though he longed to span it, he didn't know how.

But then, that wasn't exactly true. All he had to do was give himself up to this God of hers. At times he longed to do so; at others he felt a fear greater than any he had ever known. He had learned long ago that when surrendering to anyone, you then became a slave. It was that thought more than anything that kept him from taking such a drastic step.

He seated himself next to her and studied her face. She looked weary, and he wondered if sleep had eluded her as it had him. At his continued perusal, her cheeks bloomed rosily, giving at least some semblance of color to her wan face.

It had been a week since Tapat had handed over Hazaq. She had come to terms with the fact that she had done what was best for the babe long before he had. He had questioned himself over and over about whether he had done right by talking Tapat into giving the child up, but in just a week, Hazaq had put on weight and his coloring was much improved.

He picked up a stick lying on the ground close by and threw it into the water, watching as it bobbed and swirled and then tumbled to the gorge below.

"You have not been to see Hazaq," he stated.

She watched the stick moving in the water below them. Shaking her head she told him, "No. I thought it best to allow him to bond with his new mother without my interference."

He didn't know why he was surprised. If she had the courage to give the child up in the first place, then surely she was strong enough to do whatever was best to see him happy. It took a great depth of love to be able to do such a thing. An unselfish love. Something he had learned long ago that she had in abundance.

He narrowed his eyes and wrinkled his nose as he stared up at the hot Palestinian sun. They were shaded by the green overgrowth, the grass on the hillside cooling the temperatures around them. In a way, this place reminded him of Rome, except without the stench of the polluted Tiber River. He could see why the Christians had decided to settle here. It was a beautiful area.

"I haven't seen you for a few days."

He recognized the statement for the question it was. Had she missed him?

"The magistrate asked for our help. They have been having problems with the zealots invading the Decapolis and wreaking havoc on the outlying settlements. I'm assuming they are allied with the same ones that attacked us."

She didn't ask further, and he was glad. He didn't want to have to tell her about their excursions, nor the lives they had taken.

He glanced at her. "I understand you have purchased a house."

She turned to him in surprise.

"Jason told me when I came to see you. Because you

weren't at the house he indicated, he thought you might be here."

She looked around at the hills and rushing water, her face alight with her feelings. The spark that had died when she had given up Hazaq seemed to have been reignited.

"I feel closer to the Lord here than anywhere." She sighed softly.

He followed her look, nodding. "I remember you once telling me that God spoke to us through the beauty of His creation. At times like this, I can almost believe it."

The expectant look on her face brought him up short. He didn't want to give her a false hope that he believed in this God of hers. It wasn't her God that he had come to talk about, nor the beauty of the hills and trees. What he needed to say his lips were reluctant to utter.

"I have to return to Jerusalem," he finally said.

She turned to him, unable to conceal the emotions shining out from her dark eyes. He had thought for a time that she had become enamored of Crassus, but that look told him otherwise. He had experience enough with women to recognize love when he saw it. His heart began thundering in response and he forgot what he had been about to say.

He struggled with whether to accept the unintentional invitation in her eyes. It would be so easy to take advantage of her innocence, but the complete trust on her face made his baser instincts die a quick death.

"Must you?"

He noted the rapid rise and fall of her chest, which spoke of her own checked emotions. He looked away, fighting the urge to take her in his arms and show her just how much he loved her. But what good would it do? More than likely he was going to die in the coming battle and she would marry one of her Christians and live a long and happy life with a passel of children running around.

That bitter thought made him turn back to her. All of his

good intentions floated away like the stick he had thrown into the river. He couldn't die without knowing what it would be like to just once be held in her arms, not as a consoling friend but as a man, to kiss those rosy lips until they both forgot that they were mortal enemies.

He moved closer, cupping her cheeks with his palms. Her startled eyes met his. She placed her palms against his chest, but she didn't move away. Needing no further encouragement, he brought his lips down on hers.

Her inexperienced response forced him to rein in the passion that had been longing to escape for some time. Drawing on willpower he didn't know he possessed, he gentled his kisses.

Tapat had given in to the desire to be treated like a woman who loved and was loved in return. She had seen in Andronicus's eyes a desire that matched her own and, against her better judgment, had allowed his kiss.

She felt herself sinking in a maelstrom of emotion. It would be so easy to give in to the pleasure of the moment, especially knowing that it might never come again.

Oh, how she wanted to believe that he loved her as she loved him, but she had known him far too long. Too many women had come and gone in his life for her to take him seriously. He couldn't possibly understand the depth of love between a man and a woman when they came together with the Lord's blessing.

That thought was like a drenching in the cold waters of the river. She struggled against Andronicus's hold until he finally realized that she was serious and he pulled back slightly, staring in confusion into her stormy eyes.

She saw him mentally shake himself and he slowly released her. Only now did she realize that her body was trembling. He noticed, too. Turning away from her, he drew his knees up against his chest and pushed his hair back with hands that trembled much like her own. He blew out a strong gust of breath.

"I'm sorry," he told her huskily. "I shouldn't have done that."

Pain rippled through her in wave upon wave. Hadn't she already known that his feelings didn't match her own? She was just a debt to be repaid.

"Why?"

He turned to her in surprise. "What?"

"Why are you sorry?"

He opened and closed his mouth several times, reminding her of a fish out of water. Frowning, he told her, "I have no right to give you hope that there could be some kind of relationship between us."

Tapat flinched. He was only saying what she already knew; he had only done what he felt was his duty because she had once saved his life, but he was also a man with a man's desires. She turned her head so that he couldn't see how much he had hurt her. Pulling a blade of grass, she began chewing on it as she looked out over the Jordan Valley.

"It was only a kiss," she told him, surprised that her voice was steady.

Gripping her chin between his thumb and finger, he turned her to face him again. Anger darkened his cinnamon-brown eyes.

"I don't believe that! Not for someone like you."

She jerked away from him, climbing quickly to her feet. The peace she had felt earlier had long since disappeared. Another sure sign that she needed to get away from him.

"You know nothing about me!" she spat angrily. "Not really."

They glared at each other for several seconds, neither knowing what to say. All she knew was that he was leaving and she would probably never see him again. She absolutely would not break down in front of him again. "I need to go home," she told him, turning and walking away.

She heard him get to his feet and quickened her pace.

He caught up with her and pulled her around to face him, and for the first time in a long time, she felt real fear at his intimidating presence. He was every inch the affronted male.

Andronicus gripped her upper arms tightly, but seeing her flinch, he loosened his hold slightly and checked his quick temper.

"I know a lot about you," he disagreed testily. "I know you are kind and loving, generous and giving. You are beautiful inside and out." He could easily have added to the list. She was loyal to a fault. If she knew that he loved her, she would wait for him; she would wait an eternity if she had to, giving up any hope of a normal life of family and children. He couldn't do that to her. "Any man would be pleased to have you," he finished quietly.

"But I'm not for someone like you," she said softly, and he didn't bother to deny it.

"I've been a long time without a woman," he told her, rubbing salt in the wound. "Yes, I find you desirable, but you were right when you said we were too different."

He could see her fighting the tears. "Please let me go," she begged, her tear-laden voice twisting his insides.

"Tapat…"

She pushed his hands away angrily. "You've done your *duty,* now just leave me alone!"

Turning, she ran, and this time, clenching his fists against the desire to go after her, he let her go.

Tapat ran, her tears blinding her. She stumbled, picked herself up and moved on.

She had known all along that this would happen. Isn't

that exactly why the Lord had warned about being yoked with an unbeliever? And although she and Andronicus weren't married, they might as well have been because, in her heart, she knew she would never love another. They were as bound in her mind as if they had spoken the vows. She had allowed herself to love him when she had known better.

It was so easy to empathize with Andronicus's servant, Nasab. He wanted to go home to his own country, but he felt compelled by honor and duty to stay with Andronicus. She wouldn't wish that for anyone. Especially not Andronicus.

Honor and duty. What cold words when applied to a person's reason for staying with you. Andronicus had felt honor bound to bring her safely to Pella, but now that he had fulfilled his obligation, he had another duty, one that she didn't envy him at all. One that would in all probability cost him his life.

She stopped, horror washing over her. If Andronicus died, he would be lost for all eternity, sentenced to go where the lost angels who had given up their place in heaven were sent. The Lord had said that there would be no light, and there would be weeping and gnashing of teeth. Utter darkness. Incredible anguish. Gehenna was the absolute opposite of heaven, two places she had yet to discuss with Andronicus. Had Lucius? Had Anna? Did he have any idea what turning his back on Elohim would cost him?

He might not, but she did. The picture it invoked made her tremble all over. She could almost see Andronicus writhing in pain, crying out in anguish, tormented by the thought that it was for eternity and he had rejected the Savior that could have spared him. Like the rich man and Lazarus that the Lord had spoken about, she could see herself on one side of the divide and Andronicus on the other, begging for just a drop of water to quench his thirst.

Groaning at the picture in her mind, the tears that had

lessened now returned in full force. Guilt forced her to stop. How many days had they traveled together, yet she hadn't spoken of Christ and salvation to anyone except Crassus, and that was only because he'd asked.

She turned, intent on retracing her steps and remedying this oversight, but another thought stopped her. They had exchanged harsh words and she still felt defenseless against the feelings he could inspire in her just by looking at her. She wasn't certain she could cope with such emotions just now. She had come so close to losing herself in his kisses. So close. Wisdom dictated that it would be best if she kept a safe distance. Especially now.

Perhaps Crassus could reason with him where she had failed. Soldier to soldier. He would be at the gathering of believers tonight. She would talk to him about it then.

Chapter 16

Tapat hurried toward the city center, where she knew Andronicus and his men would be preparing to depart for Jerusalem. At the meeting last evening, Crassus had informed her that they would begin the return journey today. Heads close together, they had discussed ways and means of reaching Andronicus with the saving grace of Elohim's perfect love.

Crassus had impressed her with his desire to absorb everything he could about the Lord Jesus. He had sat in on the meetings every night, telling Tapat that he needed to learn as much as possible before he returned to Jerusalem.

She well understood his reasoning. He might be facing eternity in the very near future. She prayed daily that would not be so.

Last night, Jason had read from Paul's letter to the church in Rome. Crassus had hung on every word, as had Tapat. She had never heard this letter discussed before. The one statement that had remained imbedded in her memory was what Paul had said about the Lord working all things for the good of those who love Him.

In her heart she knew that, but too often her head got in her way. It was good to be reminded of the hardships Paul had faced. Even death at the hands of Nero. Yet he had remained faithful to the very end.

Crassus had left the meeting determined to reach not only his commander with the truth of Elohim's saving grace, but also the others in his group. She didn't blame Crassus for his hesitancy in approaching his commander. Andronicus was an intimidating presence at the best of times. His ability to hide his feelings behind a bland mask could be very off-putting.

Despite what had passed between Andronicus and herself, Tapat couldn't allow him to leave without wishing him Godspeed.

She found the soldiers already seated on their horses on the verge of departing and surrounded by the city's magistrates. The lead magistrate handed Andronicus a document, and then he and the others left to attend the forum.

Andronicus looked up and saw her. She couldn't miss the relief that passed through his eyes. Did he regret their last encounter as much as she did? If only they hadn't stepped beyond the bounds of friendship, they could have parted as the friends they had always been.

Crassus noticed her and smiled. He dismounted and came to her, taking her hands into his and squeezing gently. "I will miss you."

Tapat dragged her gaze away from Andronicus and focused on the young man standing before her.

"As I will you. Take care, Crassus, and may Elohim be with you."

"And you," he replied softly. Releasing her, he remounted and stood patiently awaiting the order to move out, but Andronicus gave no such command. Instead he walked his horse over to Tapat.

She looked up, an apology ready on her lips, but the words she was about to utter died at the look in his eyes. Her foolish heart responded to that look in a way that told her it refused to be repressed any longer.

"Amo te, mea vita," he said. Although she did not understand the language, his soft voice sent little thrills parading through her.

She saw his men glance at him in surprise, then quickly look away.

She frowned, ready to ask his meaning, but he continued, "May your God be with you."

Understanding dawned. He was wishing her well. She gratefully accepted the peace offering he extended.

She took a deep breath, willing herself not to be a disgrace by bursting into tears. She was beyond frustrated at her seeming penchant lately for crying at the least provocation. What had happened to her ability to bury her feelings deep inside?

"I will pray for you," she answered just as softly, and he gave a brief nod in acceptance of her return offering of peace.

They stared at each other several long seconds before his lips set in a grim line and he reined his horse about and dug in his heels. The others quickly turned their mounts and followed.

Tapat watched them galloping away until they were out of sight. She was too numb to cry anymore. Her life had taken so many unexpected twists and turns in the past two weeks, suffered so many losses, and she wasn't certain how to make herself move ahead. What was she supposed to do with her life now?

She returned to her home, stood in the doorway and looked around at the little residence she had been able to purchase with the silver Andronicus had given her. It was small yet had several rooms. It had been abandoned long ago but was still in fairly good condition. As yet, she hadn't even bothered to clean it.

She had spent every waking moment at the waterfall since giving Hazaq to his new parents; she had prayed to Elohim for hours on end before she had finally found some measure of peace. She had even forsaken the evening's assembly of believers the past several days knowing that to see Hazaq with his new mother would undo all the harmony she had managed to achieve.

That thought alone made her shut the door once again and head to her favorite spot near the waterfall. But after her time spent here with Andronicus, that place held too many unhappy memories for her to find the tranquility she was seeking.

Instead, she decided to go and find Jason. As an elder in the church, he had his finger on the pulse of the Christian community and she was looking for a new purpose in life. The thought of being idle was anathema to her. Christ asked her to serve, and serve she would until she could do so no longer.

The Apostle Paul had told the believers to rejoice in every circumstance. That didn't mean to be happy but to rejoice in the knowledge that whatever befell you, Christ would always be with you. Even the Apostle Peter had said that suffering would hone one's faith.

She smiled wryly, her whole being darkened with an ache she was trying so hard to deny. Well, if suffering would increase her faith, then surely before long she would be able to move one of the surrounding mountains.

A servant let her into Jason's house and led her to the peristyle, where she found him pottering among his flower beds.

He glanced up at her, instant sympathy creasing his elderly features. He rose and motioned her to come farther into the garden.

"Come in, child."

She swallowed back the tears that had been hovering near the surface all morning. She had shed a river of them lately, and tears never solved anyone's problems.

Jason offered her a seat on the bench near the fountain, then seated himself beside her.

"I understand Crassus and the others left this morning."

She nodded, dropping her head to allow her hair to fall forward and hide the signs of distress on her face.

That he didn't immediately answer spoke well of his wisdom. What was there to say? Surely a man of his insight had noticed her intense feelings for Andronicus.

"What can I do for you, Tapat?" he finally asked, his soft voice soothing her frayed nerves.

She focused on her fingers, twining and untwining them. "I was hoping that you might know of a way for me to do something to help the believers here."

Several seconds passed before he said, "I see."

And she had the distinct impression that he really did.

"Come with me," he said, rising and holding out his hand. "Perhaps I *do* know of something."

Tapat looked up and beheld his face, which radiated with excitement. She frowned but trustingly placed her hand into his.

Jason led her from the garden and through the atrium to the door that led onto the street, talking all the while about inconsequential trivialities. Whatever had excited him earlier he was keeping to himself.

He stopped in front of a small house in the section of the city she had learned was where most of the Christians lived. Her own house was just up the street, almost on the edge of the city.

"I want you to meet someone," he told her, knocking on the wooden door.

A tired-looking woman answered the door as she wiped her hands on a towel. Her eyes lit up when they saw Jason.

"Jason! Welcome!"

She noticed Tapat and looked at Jason in question.

"Hello, Acta. I wanted to introduce you to Tapat and introduce her to Abigail, as well."

A look of vexation crossed Acta's face. Rolling her eyes to the ceiling, she told him, "Go right ahead, but I must warn you, she's in one of her moods."

Jason smiled sympathetically, then took Tapat's arm. He led her through the small house and into a section that had obviously been added recently. The new clay was at odds with the older, faded portion of the house, which was beginning to crumble.

Only one door was in this section. Jason knocked on it.

"Go away and leave me alone."

The elderly female voice held a noticeable quaver, and Tapat glanced at Jason curiously. His halfhearted smile was hardly reassuring. He sighed.

"Abigail is a rather…difficult woman," he told her quietly. Raising his voice, he called, "Abigail, it's Jason."

This pronouncement was followed by a long silence. Jason waited patiently until he was bidden to enter in a begrudging voice.

"Come in, if you must."

Rather than be affronted, Jason grinned at Tapat's raised eyebrows. "She's quite a handful, but right now she is doing a lot of good helping those who are less fortunate."

He opened the door and went inside, Tapat following close behind.

An elderly woman sat on a sleeping couch, her straggly gray hair flying about her head in a disorderly way. She was missing most of her teeth, which made her mouth droop in a perpetual frown.

But it was her eyes that caught Tapat's attention. They were focused on Jason and they glowed with a pleasure she very much doubted he was aware of. There was something else in those faded brown orbs that Tapat doubted the others were aware of either; they were full of pain. It was the same look she had seen in so many others who were dying in the Valley of Lepers.

"Abigail," Jason said softly, "I want you to meet someone."

Suspicion suddenly flooded the old woman's face. She turned to Tapat, the welcome expression for Jason disappearing in an instant. She frowned at Tapat.

"Who is that?"

Jason gave Tapat a reassuring smile and gently pushed her toward the bed.

"Abigail, this is Tapat. She has recently come to us from Jerusalem."

Abigail's eye's opened wide at this declaration. "Jerusalem." The word came out on a longing sigh.

Tapat went closer to the bed. "You are from Jerusalem?" she asked.

Abigail's face went suddenly blank as she looked a long way into the past. "Many years ago."

She was silent several moments, lost in her own memories. Jason and Tapat waited patiently until she once more became aware of their presence.

"Don't just stand there," she snapped. "Sit down, the both of you."

Tapat seated herself on a small stool at the foot of the bed, and Jason took his place beside the bed on the only chair in the room. He reached out and took the old woman's hand.

"I can't stay, Abigail, but Tapat is looking for some way

to help others in the community and I immediately thought of you and all the good work you are doing here."

Tapat and Abigail studied each other curiously. Tapat wondered how she could help the community when it was obvious that the old woman was a cripple and in excruciating pain? It was equally obvious that those thoughts were reflected on her face and not appreciated. Abigail's frown became fiercer, if that was possible.

Jason glanced between them and recognized the storm brewing on Abigail's face. He hastily intervened.

"Show her, Abigail," he suggested.

For a moment, Tapat thought she would refuse, but then Tapat smiled her most apologetic smile in hopes that the older woman would realize that she had meant no offense in her honest appraisal. "I would love to see."

Abigail slowly pulled forth some material from beside her that Tapat hadn't noticed; it had been hidden by the blankets on her bed. She held it out to Tapat, and Tapat could see that Abigail was carefully seaming a woolen garment. Despite her age and shaking hands, the stitches were remarkably tiny and perfect. She had put a lot of work into the garment, making it not only serviceable but also beautiful. Impressed, Tapat glanced from the garment back to Abigail.

Once again perceptively reading the look on Tapat's face, Abigail visibly relaxed at the honest respect she saw there.

"Do you sell these?"

Jason answered for her. "No, she sews garments and gives them to the, shall we say, less affluent here."

"Jason provides the material," Abigail inserted, intent on making certain that credit was given where credit was due.

Tapat was surprised that a man of Jason's age could still blush.

With instant empathy, Tapat understood; loneliness was

relieved by being of service to others. How tedious it must be to be confined to a small room day in and day out, nothing to do but try to ignore the increasing pain that age was forcing on the body. The longing for companionship was evident in Abigail's fading brown eyes.

The ache in Tapat's heart lessened in light of this revelation. She looked from Jason to Abigail. "How can I be of help? Although I can sew, my stitches would be ashamed to be seen in the presence of such skill."

Abigail sat up straighter, her chest puffing out at the praise.

Jason chuckled. "Abigail would be able to accomplish much more if she had someone to be her legs."

"My son is too busy with his own tailor business, and my daughter-in-law..." She hesitated at the look of reproach that Jason gave her, but Tapat hadn't missed the bitterness in her voice. "My daughter-in-law is too busy with her housekeeping."

Tapat got up from the stool and went and sat next to Abigail on the bed. She felt drawn to this old woman who helped others despite her own adversity. Jason stood and, looking down on both of them, gave them a beatific smile.

"I have some business that I need to attend to, so I will leave you two to get better acquainted." He squeezed Abigail's frail hand. "Tapat will bring you more supplies later. A caravan passed by a few days ago and I was able to purchase some wonderful material they had brought from the East."

Gratitude shone from the old woman's eyes, but she merely nodded.

Tapat and Abigail watched him leave, then turned to mutually study each other. Tapat knew she had found a friend.

Chapter 17

For Tapat, the days fell into a pattern. In the morning she made her breakfast and memorized the portion of Paul's letter to the Romans, which Jason had allowed her to copy. She then spent an hour in prayer before going to Abigail's and helping her sew garments. Because Abigail was unable, Tapat would then hand them out to the poor in the community.

If the ache in her heart was apparent to the old woman, she never said, but Tapat noticed that Abigail frequently watched her with knowing and sympathetic eyes.

Tapat had learned that Abigail didn't exactly dislike her daughter-in-law; they just didn't understand each other.

Acta was a Roman through and through. She worshipped the gods of the Greeks and Romans, often staring in exasperation at Abigail and Tapat for what she considered their foolish religion.

Abigail's son had drifted away from his Jewish faith, refusing to step into the confrontations between his wife and his mother. He chose another path—the way of the agnostic, which was insidiously creeping into the minds of many.

Watching their relationship, Tapat could better understand why the Lord had forbidden his children to be yoked with unbelievers. Not that there was a lack of love. On the contrary, Acta and her husband were forever smiling at each other, touching when they thought no one was looking. Despite the disparity in their beliefs, Tapat envied them that love, but she wondered how much better their life would be if they plowed in the same direction instead of pulling against each other.

As for Jason and Tapat, Acta readily accepted them for the relief they brought from caring for her mother-in-law.

Tapat thought it a shame that Acta's attitude had affected her three children, who had no time for their own grandmother. It was no wonder that Abigail had grown bitter in her loneliness.

Because Abigail's son, David, was Jewish and Acta was Roman, Tapat, head bent over her stitching, asked Abigail about her conversion to the Way. The older woman smiled, her eyes taking on a faraway look.

"It was Jason's doing," she said. Tapat stopped stitching at something in Abigail's voice. She looked at Tapat. "Have you ever heard of demons?"

Tapat had heard the stories of demons and demon possession. She wasn't exactly sure where Abigail was going with this, but it was as though a shadow suddenly passed over the sun. Tapat felt a chill shiver through her.

"Jason used to live in Gergesa, an area close to the Sea of Galilee," Abigail told her, never interrupting her close stitching. "He was possessed by a legion of demons and used to roam through the graveyards and hills close to the sea."

Tapat forgot altogether about sewing. The garment she was working on lay forgotten on her lap as she listened, enthralled, to the story Abigail told her. It was truly hard to believe. Jason would have been just a young man then, but even so, she was having a hard time accepting that he could break chains and overturn boulders. It was hard for her mind to take in.

"And then Jesus came to him one night and, even though he was a Gentile, cast the demons out. They went into a herd of pigs, ran into the sea and drowned."

Tapat didn't know what to say.

"Jason asked Jesus if he could follow Him, but the Lord told him to go home and tell his family what had happened. It wasn't yet time for the Lord to show that He had come to bring salvation to the Gentiles as well as the Jews. Jason did tell his family, but he didn't stop there. He traveled all over the Decapolis telling his story. Some people, those who had known of Jason, believed. Others did not."

"And you?"

She stopped sewing, once more staring off into space. "I heard him speak in the forum one day and believed what he had to say. The Greeks don't understand demons, nor even Satan, but, as a Jew, I had no trouble believing all of it. The hard part for me was accepting that the Messiah had finally come. Being a Gentile, Jason had no idea just who Jesus was, so I explained the Messiah to him."

"How came you to live in the Decapolis?" Tapat asked curiously.

Abigail sighed. "When David married Acta, he was shunned by the Jews in Jerusalem. It became hard for him to make a living, except among the Gentiles who were much more lenient in regards to such matters. He had heard about the Decapolis and, though the area has clung to its Greek heritage, it has become a gathering of nationalities."

Abigail tied off her finishing seam and bit the threads. Shaking out the garment, she checked for any flaws. Tapat knew she wouldn't find any.

Abigail laid the garment in her lap, staring out the small window that overlooked the green hills that surrounded Pella.

"My husband died many years ago, so I live with my son. When he moved here, I came along."

Something in her voice made Tapat look at her closely.

"When I became a Christian, he was angry, but there was little he could say when he had married a Gentile himself."

Tapat knew that David wasn't of the Way, but she had to give him credit for continuing to support his mother. He might reject the Savior she had come to believe in, but he would never reject his mother. Which was probably why he refused to get embroiled in arguments between his wife and his mother. It was obvious that he loved them both.

Abigail handed over the garment she had been working on. "This one goes to little Hector," she told Tapat.

Tapat smiled. Hector was a small boy who had been crippled in an accident several years ago. Even though he had to walk on crutches, he was a joy to be around, always looking on the bright side of life.

She kissed the old woman on the cheek, smiling as her wrinkled face colored in embarrassment.

"Go on with you," Abigail snorted, but Tapat didn't miss the sparkle in her faded old eyes.

Saying goodbye to Acta and getting a brisk nod in return, Tapat wished again that there was some way to reach the woman and her husband for the Lord. It would make life so much more joyful for everyone in that house.

After she had finished handing out the garments, she made her way to the waterfall and seated herself next to the flowing water. When she came here now, she no longer felt the sadness of her parting from Andronicus; she felt only the peace of Elohim that only the beauty of His world could inspire.

This was her praying spot. Many hours she had spent here praying for everyone she could think of, including herself.

Days had turned into weeks, weeks into months. Loneliness and sadness still dogged her days, and if she wasn't entirely happy, she was at least content.

It had taken time, but she had eventually been able to bring herself to hold Hazaq again and be happy for the life he had found. When she returned him to his mother, the emptiness of her arms stayed with her long after she returned to her own home.

She threw a stick into the water, remembering when Andronicus had done the very same thing. She watched it bobbing along until it fell over the waterfall. Soon this small stream would become a rushing torrent. It was now the month of Elul, what the Romans called August. In another month, the first rains would begin and the wadis would once again run with water, the life-giving source for much of the region.

"Tapat! Tapat!"

Startled, Tapat turned to see little Hector struggling to hurry to her, greatly impeded by his crutches. She got to her feet and hastened to him, the excitement in his voice bringing a rush of fear.

He reached her, struggling to regain his breath and talk at the same time.

She knelt before him, gently clasping his thin upper arms. "Calm yourself, Hector. Catch your breath before you try to speak."

He did as she asked, finally taking a deep breath and letting it out slowly.

"A messenger has come," he told her, his voice gaining pitch as the exciting news he was about to share caught up with him again. "Jerusalem has fallen!"

Tapat went cold all over. How was this possible in so

short of a time? It had only been two months since she had left Jerusalem.

"Are you certain that is what the messenger said?" she asked, her heart pounding with dread.

He nodded vigorously.

"What else did he say?"

Hector shrugged. "I didn't stay to hear. I came to find you."

Tapat picked up his crutch, which had fallen to the ground, and handed it back to him. Holding on to his other arm, she turned him around. "Let's go and find out exactly what has happened."

As usual when something unusual happened, everyone gathered at Jason's villa to discuss it. His was the only house large enough to fit all of the believers at one time.

She listened as the messenger told about the destruction of the temple. Although Tapat knew that the Lord no longer lived in such temples, she still felt a great sadness for the loss of a symbol that had always been an integral part of her people's choice to follow the one true God.

And what of Andronicus and Crassus? Would she ever know what had happened to them?

Dejected, she left the meeting and went to share the information with Abigail. The old woman would be heartbroken.

It was a week later, and Tapat was once again helping Abigail. Tapat overheard Acta and David talking about David's trip to Caesarea Maritima. He tailored garments to ship to a merchant in Rome and he needed to oversee it personally.

Through the open door she could see Acta helping him pack the goods he needed to take and sniffing back tears. David's handsome face gentled with concern as he brushed the tears from her cheeks.

"I won't be gone long," he told her softly.

"But the zealots…"

He placed a finger over her lips. "I will be fine. Expect me to return before the next moon."

She kissed his finger. *"Amo te."*

He pulled her into a hug. "I love you, too. Take care of my mother while I am gone."

Tapat sat frozen, her face leaching of color. Abigail frowned at her.

"Are you all right?"

Tapat sucked in a deep breath, eyes blinking rapidly as she tried to digest what she had just overheard. "I'll be right back. I need to ask Acta something."

Acta was standing at the door watching David as he disappeared into the distance. She finally turned back inside, frowning when she saw Tapat standing behind her. She hastily brushed the remaining tears from her cheeks.

"What do you want?"

Tapat ignored her belligerence. "What does *amo te* mean?"

Acta's frown deepened. "You were listening?"

"Not intentionally," Tapat disagreed. "It's just that I've heard that phrase before. I thought it was a statement of goodwill."

Acta laughed, studying Tapat with a look that could only be considered insulting.

"It means *I love you.*"

Tapat's heart began thudding in her chest. "And *mea vita?*"

"Where did you hear that?" she asked curiously.

"From one of the soldiers I was traveling with," Tapat told her. "What does it mean?"

Acta pushed past her and went to the table to begin kneading the dough she had set earlier. "It means *my life.*"

Tapat stood like a statue as she remembered the incident with Andronicus looking down at her from the height of his horse.

Amo te, mea vita, he had said softly.

"I love you, my life," Tapat whispered, her thoughts raging out of control.

"What did you say?" Acta asked, glaring at her suspiciously.

Tapat shook her head. "Nothing. Nothing at all," she answered, going back into Abigail's room and seating herself in the chair by the bed. She picked up the garment she had been working on, but it lay forgotten on her lap as her mind continued to whirl.

"Are you all right?" Abigail asked again, her concerned voice bringing Tapat's mind back into focus. "You are as white as the snow that covers the mountains in winter."

"I…I…" Tapat got swiftly to her feet, replacing the garment on the bed. "I'm sorry, Abigail. There's something I have to do."

She hurried from the room, ignoring Acta's curious stare as she left the house. She needed time alone. Time to think and pray.

Could it be true? Did Andronicus truly love her? How was that even possible?

She climbed up the hill to the waterfall, dropping to the ground and curling her legs under her. She was having trouble getting her thoughts into some kind of logical order to know how to pray.

The thought uppermost in her mind was whether Andronicus had survived the attack on Jerusalem. If he loved her, could that have been why he led her to think otherwise? She pushed her palms against her temples and groaned as she tried to stop the images dancing trough her mind. She fell prostrate on the ground and prayed harder, not really knowing what she was saying, just allowing her spirit to speak her agony to the Lord.

How long she lay thus, she was uncertain. The shadows were beginning to lengthen, letting her know that darkness would soon be covering the land. She really needed to head home, but it was so peaceful here. She could hear the doves cooing as they settled themselves in the trees for the night. The rushing water tumbling and gurgling over the rocks was amplified in the stillness.

Skittering rocks on the hill behind her let her know that someone or something was approaching. She sat up, wiping from her cheeks the tears that she hadn't even known she had shed.

When Andronicus came into view, her heart stuttered and then began racing faster than a speeding chariot. She slowly got to her feet, wanting nothing more than to run to him and throw herself into his arms. At her hesitation, he stopped, then slowly resumed walking toward her.

When he was close enough, he reached up and pushed a lock of hair behind her ear, his eyes intent as they searched her face.

"I made a promise to myself that if God would spare my life, I would come back for you."

She stared at him, stupefied. What was he saying? Which god was he talking about?

He sighed heavily and wrapped her in arms of steel, his hold so tight it restricted her breathing, but she didn't care. She hoped he would never let her go. He laid his cheek against the top of her head.

"There is so much I have to tell you," he said, his deep voice that she had thought never to hear again sending little thrills of pleasure dancing through her.

"Tell me, then," she encouraged.

He pulled back, giving her a look that nearly melted her bones.

"Let's sit down."

She readily complied, her legs so shaky she didn't think

they would hold her. She seated herself where she could watch his face as he talked.

"Where do I begin?" he asked, almost to himself. "Many of the things you spoke to me about came back to me, often at the strangest times."

He began by telling her about the attack on Jerusalem and how, in the thick of battle, he had noticed that Crassus seemed to be protected by some kind of invisible shield. Attacked on all sides, he fought with a strength that seemed to be beyond him.

"It was amazing," he told her, the intensity of his voice making her shiver. "Even Titus, after seeing the strength and fortifications of Jerusalem, said that we could not have done it without the help of your God," Andronicus told her. "And I remembered what you had said about the Jews turning their backs on His Son, and I thought to myself, 'Are we then God's avenging messenger?'"

She held her breath, awed by the things he had to say.

"Then, when your beautiful temple was destroyed, I remembered what you had said about your God no longer living in a temple but in the hearts of mankind." His voice deepened with feeling. "It's the one thing that Rome cannot understand. You can destroy and perhaps enslave a people, but you cannot destroy an idea."

He stopped, turning to her and staring hard into her eyes.

"At night, I looked up at the stars and remembered what you had said about them showing the handiwork of your God. It made sense, in a way. Despite everything going on around, all the chaos, all the killing, the world continued as it has for all time. It made me realize just how little man is in the whole scheme of things. Civilizations come, and civilizations go. Emperors come, and emperors go. But the world goes on unchanged. Like God."

She searched deep into his eyes with a question that she was afraid to ask.

"I stopped on the way here to see Jason. We had a long talk and I asked him to baptize me in the Jordan River. I remembered what you said about Christians preferring to be baptized in *living* water."

The look he gave her told her he still didn't understand much of her Christian faith, but his hesitation was swallowed up in her joyous eyes.

"You were baptized?" she questioned in a soft whisper.

He nodded, his look serious. "I didn't want to come to you until I knew that my soul was clean."

"Oh, Andronicus," she cried, throwing her arms around his neck. "Praise Elohim."

This time when he wrapped her in his arms, she didn't hold back. She boldly kissed him with a heart overflowing with joy.

Andronicus returned her kisses, a desire he had never felt before with any other woman sweeping through him. So this was what it was like to love and be loved as God intended. In Tapat's arms, he felt like he had finally come home.

He had to pull on reserves of strength to finally set Tapat away from him when all he really wanted to do was hold her forever. His shaking hands gave mute testimony to the control he was enforcing on himself.

"I still have much to learn, *mea amo.*"

Her eyes glistened with her happiness. "I will help you. We will learn together."

He studied every inch of her face, that face that had dwelled in his dreams for years. Could any woman be more beautiful? He thanked God for bringing her into his life.

"I asked Titus to relieve me of duty, and he has agreed. Now I can at last ask you to be my wife."

Her eyes glistened in the waning light, and he once

more wrapped her in his arms. Her smile almost stopped his heart.

"I love you, Tapat," he whispered. "Will you marry me?"

She leaned her head back against his arm until she could see his face clearly in the encroaching darkness. *"Amo te, mea vita,"* she told him in return, and his heart reacted furiously to her husky voice.

He was no fool. He knew that there would still be challenges ahead. She knew it, as well. But as long as they were together, they could face anything.

She pulled his head down and, with her lips, gave him her answer.

* * * * *

REQUEST YOUR FREE BOOKS!

2 FREE CHRISTIAN NOVELS
PLUS 2
FREE
MYSTERY GIFTS

HEARTSONG
PRESENTS

YES! Please send me 2 Free Heartsong Presents novels and my 2 FREE mystery gifts (gifts are worth about $10). After receiving them, if I don't wish to receive any more books I can return the shipping statement marked "cancel." If I don't cancel, I will receive 4 brand-new novels every month and be billed just $4.24 per book in the U.S. and $5.24 per book in Canada. That's a savings of at least 20% off the cover price. It's quite a bargain! Shipping and handling is just 50¢ per book in the U.S. and 75¢ per book in Canada.* I understand that accepting the 2 free books and gifts places me under no obligation to buy anything. I can always return a shipment and cancel at any time. Even if I never buy another book, the two free books and gifts are mine to keep forever.

159/359 HDN FVYK

Name _____ (PLEASE PRINT) _____

Address _____ Apt. # _____

City _____ State _____ Zip _____

Signature (if under 18, a parent or guardian must sign)

Mail to the Harlequin® Reader Service:
IN U.S.A.: P.O. Box 1867, Buffalo, NY 14240-1867

* Terms and prices subject to change without notice. Prices do not include applicable taxes. Sales tax applicable in N.Y. This offer is limited to one order per household. Not valid for current subscribers to Heartsong Presents books. All orders subject to credit approval. Credit or debit balances in a customer's account(s) may be offset by any other outstanding balance owed by or to the customer. Please allow 4 to 6 weeks for delivery. Offer available while quantities last. Offer valid only in the U.S.

REQUEST YOUR FREE BOOKS!

2 FREE INSPIRATIONAL NOVELS
PLUS 2
FREE
MYSTERY GIFTS

Love Inspired

LIDIR13R

REQUEST YOUR FREE BOOKS!

2 FREE INSPIRATIONAL NOVELS
PLUS 2
FREE
MYSTERY GIFTS

Love Inspired.

HISTORICAL
INSPIRATIONAL HISTORICAL ROMANCE

YES! Please send me 2 FREE Love Inspired® Historical novels and my 2 FREE mystery gifts (gifts are worth about $10). After receiving them, if I don't wish to receive any more books, I can return the shipping statement marked "cancel." If I don't cancel, I will receive 4 brand-new novels every month and be billed just $4.74 per book in the U.S. or $5.24 per book in Canada. That's a savings of at least 21% off the cover price. It's quite a bargain! Shipping and handling is just 50¢ per book in the U.S. and 75¢ per book in Canada.* I understand that accepting the 2 free books and gifts places me under no obligation to buy anything. I can always return a shipment and cancel at any time. Even if I never buy another book, the two free books and gifts are mine to keep forever.

102/302 IDN F5CY

Name _____ (PLEASE PRINT) _____

Address _____ Apt. #

City _____ State/Prov. _____ Zip/Postal Code

Signature (if under 18, a parent or guardian must sign)

Mail to the Harlequin® Reader Service:
IN U.S.A.: P.O. Box 1867, Buffalo, NY 14240-1867
IN CANADA: P.O. Box 609, Fort Erie, Ontario L2A 5X3

Want to try two free books from another series?
Call 1-800-873-8635 or visit www.ReaderService.com.

* Terms and prices subject to change without notice. Prices do not include applicable taxes. Sales tax applicable in N.Y. Canadian residents will be charged applicable taxes. Offer not valid in Quebec. This offer is limited to one order per household. Not valid for current subscribers to Love Inspired Historical books. All orders subject to credit approval. Credit or debit balances in a customer's account(s) may be offset by any other outstanding balance owed by or to the customer. Please allow 4 to 6 weeks for delivery. Offer available while quantities last.

Your Privacy—The Harlequin® Reader Service is committed to protecting your privacy. Our Privacy Policy is available online at www.ReaderService.com or upon request from the Harlequin Reader Service.

We make a portion of our mailing list available to reputable third parties that offer products we believe may interest you. If you prefer that we not exchange your name with third parties, or if you wish to clarify or modify your communication preferences, please visit us at www.ReaderService.com/consumerschoice or write to us at Harlequin Reader Service Preference Service, P.O. Box 9062, Buffalo, NY 14269. Include your complete name and address.

ReaderService.com

Manage your account online!

- Review your order history
- Manage your payments
- Update your address

*We've designed
the Harlequin® Reader Service
website just for you.*

Enjoy all the features!

- Reader excerpts from any series
- Respond to mailings and special monthly offers
- Discover new series available to you
- Browse the Bonus Bucks catalog
- Share your feedback

Visit us at:
ReaderService.com

RS13